THE FIREWALKERS

BY THE SAME AUTHOR

FRANCIS KING

THE FIREWALKERS

First published 1956 by John Murray (Publishers) Ltd.
This edition and Introduction
published 1985 as a Gay Modern Classic
by GMP Publishers Ltd,
P O Box 247, London N15 6RW.

Copyright © Francis King 1956
Introduction copyright © Francis King 1985

Distributed in North America by
Alyson Publications Inc.,
40 Plympton Street, Boston, MA 02118, USA.

British Library Cataloguing in Publication Data

King, Francis, *1923-*
The Firewalkers. – (Gay Modern Classics)
I. Title II. Series
823'.914 [F]   PR6061.I45

ISBN 0-907040-72-1
ISBN 0-907040-71-3 Pbk

Printed and bound by Billing & Sons Ltd, Worcester, England

Introduction

When, in obedience to a regulation of the time, I submitted the manuscript of this *jeu d'esprit* to my then employers, the British Council, I was faced with an ultimatum. I could resign and publish the book under my own name; I could stay in the British Council and publish it under another name; or I could stay in the British Council and not publish it at all. It was clear that it was the last of these three alternatives that the Council favoured.

There were two reasons for this severity. The first — and how ludicrous it seems in these libertarian days, nearly thirty years later — was that the book dealt (as one of the British Council officers responsible for acting as its censors put it to me) with 'murky and, to many people, distasteful aspects of sexuality'. The second was that it was all too plainly a *roman à clef*.

I opted to remain in the British Council — where I continued for a further decade — and to publish the book under a pseudonym. Why Frank Cauldwell? Cauldwell had been the maiden name of one of my great-grandmothers; but, more important, Frank Cauldwell had been the name of the young man, in many ways identifiable with myself, who was one of the characters in my first (and, since it contained an incident of fellatio, then considered shocking) novel *To the Dark Tower*. I was vain enough to wish to leave a clue to my identity for anyone who cared enough to discover it. No one did.

Some of my close friends were, of course, privy to the secret. I was nervous that one of these, the flamboyant prototype of my central character Colonel Grecos, might react to my representation of him either with a ferocious row, of the kind that he always relished, or with a libel action. Fortunately, he adopted neither of these courses but, instead, marched around Athens, the book tucked under a bony elbow, to announce to everyone whom he met: 'I have been immortalised in a book.' As subsequent events have shown, he was in no need of immortalisation. Clearly born immortal, he can still be encountered in Athens, not a day older than when I first met him at the firewalking ceremony with which my novel opens. Though no one who does not know him will believe this, my portrait of him is composed without the smallest exaggeration.

Another character, Mrs Tullett, was an amalgamation of two Englishwomen then living in Athens, who – like many people who share basic traits – could not abide each other. When the book appeared, one of the couple, X, remarked to me: 'I loved your book. But weren't you just a little bit naughty about poor Y?' I then encountered Y, who said to me: 'I loved your book. But weren't you a little bit naughty about poor X?'

Cecil was based on Arthur Jefferies, a rich, cosmopolitan American, who owned a London gallery devoted to the work of primitive artists and who, in a fit of depression brought on by his expulsion from Venice, where he had lived in reginal splendour, took the wholly unnecessary step of killing himself. I now see that my fictional portrait, executed so many years before that tragic event, brings out the self-disgust and self-destruction then latent in him like the virus of a fatal illness.

Lady Aaronson derived from Dorothy Mayer, a writer of historical biographies, also now dead, who was the first wife of Sir Robert Mayer, founder of the Robert Mayer Concerts for Children. A charming German photographer and artist, Jo von Kalkreuth – I still treasure a small painting of two Greek sailors, arms around each other's waists, that he presented to me when I was languishing in hospital – gave me the idea for Götz. Sophie Landerlöst was based on the wife of Sir Clifford Norton, then 'our man in Athens'. Her nude bathing party really took place, at a time when naturism, like homosexuality, was generally regarded as at best comic and at worst immoral. Lady Norton had an admirably robust contempt for convention, which endeared her to the Greeks.

Other real-life people make brief appearances under their own names. Among these are Moore Crossthwaite, subsequently 'our man in Beirut'; Daphne (Lady) Bath, later Daphne Fielding, writer of sprightly biographies; and Dora Stratou, founder and directrice of a Greek folk-dance company.

Rereading the book after so many years, I once again experienced the exhilarating sense of liberation that came to me, a prim and prudish young man all but garotted by my invisible stiff-collar of upper-middle-class English do's and dont's, on first setting foot in an Athens not yet ruined by tourism and the greed and rudeness that tourism engenders. When I returned to England on my first leave, Angus Wilson remarked to me at a party: 'You've become a different person.' 'Different? How?' I asked. 'You've come out of your refrigerator,' he replied.

My experience in publishing a book under a pseudonym was the exact opposite of Doris Lessing's in the case of her recent 'Joan Somers' novels — first turned down by a number of publishers and then cold-shouldered by critics previously enthusiastic about any work that bore her own name. I was not of course as famous as Doris Lessing — nor, indeed and alas, am I now. But my first three books had been praised sufficiently highly — on the basis of them Charles Snow chose me as one of his 'six bright hopes' for the future — for my fourth, *The Dark Glasses*, to be treated sniffily. Clearly, some people thought that I was getting above myself. In contrast, when *The Firewalkers* appeared as a first novel by someone totally unknown, all the reviewers went out of their way to be kind and generous.

Many years after the publication of *The Firewalkers* — which appeared, incidentally, under the courageous imprint of John Murray and not of my normal publishers, Longmans, who were as nervous of it as the British Council — I went to a cocktail party given by Harry Morris, an old friend, now dead. Harry brought over to me a young-old man in a dark-grey suit, with sleek, carefully parted hair. The young-old man was, Harry told me, a Foreign Office colleague of his, who had recently been *en poste* in Athens. 'Are you the Francis King who wrote *The Man on the Rock?*', he asked. The aggressive tone should have warned me. I confessed that I was. 'I read it the other day and I'm afraid I must tell you that I don't think you've understood Greece and the Greeks *at all*.' I tried to appear neither rattled nor nettled, but my face must have looked like that of a mother who has just been told that her child is a monster. Then he went on: 'Now there's one novel about Greece and the Greeks that really *gets* them. You won't have heard of it. I found it quite by chance in a church jumble-sale in our village. It's called *The Firewalkers*. Do look out for it.' 'I wrote it,' I said. But of course he did not believe me, and I had to call Harry over for confirmation.

That my little book 'really *gets*' Greece and the Greeks in all their extraordinary diversity is something that I myself should never claim for it. Rather, I see it as an album of snapshots, taken in the brilliant sunshine of Athens before its Smog Age set in and of my new-found liberation at the moment when my personal Smog Age had dissipated. The snapshots will, I hope, convey something both of a vanished paradise and of a vanished self.

Francis King

CHAPTER

I

THIS is a story, not about myself, but about an old Greek and an ugly German who seemed to have nothing in common but their poverty and an unsatisfied craving to be loved. It is also a story about exile: that exile from country or class which people choose in order not to have to pay the debt of conformity which country or class exacts from them. Of such people Theodore Grecos and Götz Joachim—and indeed myself—seem to be typical representatives.

The three of us first came together one Ascension Day at a village called Langada in Macedonia, where we had each gone separately to see a religious sect, the Anastan-arides, walking on fire. I had borrowed a bicycle to cover the twelve miles out from Salonica and since these were Greek roads I inevitably arrived late. However, since these were also Greek firewalkers, my lateness did not matter. As I stepped off my bicycle—or, rather, was flung off it—in a square where the mud had been worn by farm-carts into ridges and then baked hard by the sun, a 'Hey, Johnny' approached.

'Hello, boy,' he shouted.

Perhaps when I am ten years older I shall not mind being called boy; now I dislike it.

'Hello,' I answered coldly.

He was like any old Macedonian peasant, but for the expansiveness of his manner, his obviously transatlantic tie and the wide-brimmed brown felt hat which he wore on the back of his head. He had on a black suit, a gold chain looping from one pocket of the waistcoat to another across his paunch, and a pair of heavy brown boots. The ring on his wedding finger had a diamond in it.

'You come for the firewalking?'

'Yes. Has it begun yet?'

'Begun? Say, are you joking, boy?'

'They told me it would begin at eleven.'

'You come with me. I bring you to the house of the Anastanarides.'

He approached the bicycle and I thought he was going to take it from me; but, instead, he began to ease himself cautiously on to the cross-bar until, satisfied, he exclaimed: 'O.K., boy! Let's go.' I was already sweating and breathless from the twelve miles I had covered, but I pushed off and somehow managed to keep the bicycle moving in the direction I was told. We must have looked curious, the old man sitting dignified and benign, while I panted and swore behind him, occasionally putting a leg to the ground as the bicycle jolted over.

Eventually we reached a courtyard, full of cars, people, policemen and dogs: 'All right, mister! Stop! Stop!' But the brakes on the bicycle had never functioned properly and we ended up on top of two large Salonica women in black who were seated glumly on a couple of straight-backed wooden chairs, waiting for something

2

to happen. Outraged, they continued to smooth their skirts with podgy heavily be-ringed hands for at least five minutes after the accident. I looked about me. The American Consul had climbed into a tree from which he was taking snapshots and a number of bedraggled children were peering into the windows of the car in which the French Consul and his family were eating either a late breakfast or an early lunch. 'Plenty people,' my old man said; and a priest who came to my literature classes hurried over to explain: 'Everyone is here because the Bishop said that the Anastanarides are heretics and no one should come.'

'Ought you to be here?'

'I am here as an observer,' he replied in dignified reproof.

I remembered the story of the last time a priest had been present as an observer at the ceremony. He was from the village itself, and he had taken his wife with him to support him as he delivered a solemn address to the assembled villagers on the sin of such idolatrous practices. But suddenly, as the Anastanarides danced over the fire to the sound of pipes and drums, the devil entered into his wife and she was away too, capering over the red-hot cinders, her shoes and stockings off and her skirt above her knees. That night the priest chased her with an axe, and the next morning the villagers chased them both from the village because of the scandal.

'Come, mister! You want to see inside the house?'

I had noticed that around the courtyards there were a number of shacks, roofed with either corrugated iron or bamboos, and into one of these I was now taken, after my 'Hey, Johnny' had explained in Greek to the two policemen at the door that I was an important member of the British Embassy staff. I only hoped that the two policemen had not witnessed our arrival on the ramshackle bicycle. There was only one room in the hut, and it was full of the smoke of incense so that, at first, I had nothing but an impression of vague, cow-like forms slumped around the walls while before an ikon there was kneeling a figure of an almost superhuman stature. Apart from the smell of the incense, there were the smells of human bodies, of smoke and wet clothes (it had been raining in the early morning). Everyone was murmuring but it was impossible to tell whether in conversation or prayer. My 'Hey, Johnny' said in a loud voice: 'These people, no education—no education at all! Dirty! Pah!'

The figure kneeling before the ikon turned and hissed: 'Sh!'; and I at once realised that this was not a Greek but a Northerner.

The most important fact about Götz Joachim then, as now, seemed to me to be his quite extraordinary ugliness. I have met other men who were grubby or had harelips or bit their fingernails till they bled, and yet were not repulsive; so that perhaps it was merely the combination of all these physical defects that made it so difficult for one to look at him for long. Women, who are often attracted by ugliness, recoiled from him in horror; and I noticed that male Greeks, who are always patting one in a comradely fashion, never patted Götz. As he turned round to hiss at us, it was of course his harelip that first caught my notice; then his extraordinary, wayward nose, which seemed to have been broken twice

4

in such a way that one nostril was now double the size of the other; and finally his colouring, of that albino whiteness that seems almost pink—pink hair, pink eyebrows, pink eyelashes. He was wearing a tartan windjacket, under which one could see a roll-top sailor's jersey, blue jeans so tight that it looked as if his enormous buttocks would at any moment burst the seams, and a pair of brown canvas gym-shoes through one of which a toe could be seen protruding. He now returned to his devotions with what was an obviously genuine piety: kissing the ikon, crossing himself and lighting a candle for which he dropped a thousand drachmae note into the chipped kitchen pie-dish that had been placed there for this purpose. At last he hoisted himself upright, hitting his head on the ceiling so that the corrugated iron sheet rumbled like thunder, again crossed himself and joined the entranced forms slumped around the smoke-blackened walls.

'Hey, Marika,' my friend shouted at an old woman in Greek. 'When are you going to dance?'

The old woman patted the mud floor, on which she was squatting, with a shrivelled claw: 'When the Lord bids us.'

'She says they dance when God tells them to dance,' the 'Hey, Johnny' explained. 'These very ignorant people.'

'Sh!' The German was glancing up at us through the cloud of incense with such an intensity that I at once hurried out of the hut, into the rain, that had again begun to spin across the courtyard.

'You want to hear lecture?' The 'Hey, Johnny' pursued me indefatigably. 'No good here. You get wet.'

'What lecture?'

'Colonel Grecos—he come from Athens. He talk about Anastanarides. In the village school. He very clever guy. But you no understand.'

'I've been in Greece for two years.'

'Never mind! I translate for you. Where's that son-of-a-bitch of a bicycle?'

This was my chance. I had spotted the bicycle in the hands of some children who were taking it in turns to wheel each other round on it, and calling out ' Goodbye! Thank you!' I raced towards it, grabbed it and pedalled off before I could be followed. The last I heard from my friend was a despairing shout of 'Hey, Johnny! Hey!'

In the schoolroom there were the same odours of human bodies, smoke and wet clothes; but instead of incense there was the smell of the overflowing drain across which I had had to leap in order to get in. I perched myself on top of a desk beside an old man huddled deep into a vast sheep-skin jacket, and then looked at the platform, only to grow uncomfortably conscious that the lecturer was in turn looking at me, having stopped speaking to do so. My first impression was of a personal dignity so great as really to be formidable. He was not a handsome man—his nose was too long, and the girlishly pointed chin was inappropriate under the massive cast of the rest of his features—but he was a man at whom one could look with admiration, wherever one met him. His complexion was bad, being of the colour and texture of gruyère cheese, with warts instead of holes in it; his close-clipped hair was white and stiff, and his white eyebrows bristled as thick as his moustache. He was wearing a threadbare but well-cut suit of grey flannel, which had sea-shells sewn on it in place of buttons; instead of a tie, a scarf, navy blue with the figures of sailors on it, was knotted jauntily about his long, scrawny neck. He made extravagant gestures as he talked, waving both of his hands. Altogether the effect he made was at once absurd, impressive and touching in a way one could not explain.

He was talking about the pagan origins of the fire-walking ceremonies—the Anastanarides were refugees from Thrace and there were many similarities between theirs and the ancient Orphic rites—but though he spoke well, in the resonantly produced voice of an actor or trained public speaker, and the subject itself was one which interested me, yet I was tired after the unaccustomed exertion of the bicycle ride, the room was hot and airless, and the old man by my side had already set me the example of dropping off to sleep. I began by crouching forward, then I put my forehead on my clasped hands, finally I shut my eyes. I hoped that I would not grunt and snuffle like my neighbour, and that a thread of saliva would not trickle down my chin.

I was woken by a hand squeezing my shoulder:

'Frank! What are you doing here?' a voice was whispering. I shook my head from side to side, as a dog does to get the water out of its ears. 'Come outside for God's sake. I've had enough of this. It couldn't be more boring.'

'Cecil!'

'Sh! Come outside.'

But it was impossible to get out without creating a

7

disturbance; and though I am certain Cecil Provender was willing to do so, I myself did not have the courage.

'We can't,' I said. 'Look at all those people. It won't be long now.'

'You don't know Theo.'

'Theo?'

'The old thing on the platform. It was he who had this mad idea of coming up here. It would be hard to think of anything less gay.'

'Have you been in Greece long?'

'Long enough, my dear. I think either one likes Italy or one likes Greece. Rarely both. . . . Can't you move up a little? I'm practically sitting in this old boy's lap.' I shifted along the desk and Cecil made himself more comfortable. 'Yes, I've been here about five weeks. . . . Now don't be hurt that I never got in touch with you!' So far from being hurt, I was feeling relieved. 'You know that I don't write letters, but only last night in Salonica I told Theo that we must find out where you were. Actually we were going along to your Consul or Council or whatever it is when something *distracted* this old girl.'

'Oh.'

I hoped Cecil would not begin to tell me what form the distraction took; but he was going on: 'Yes, it was just as we were coming out of that dreary restaurant on the seafront, and all at once goose-girl saw this . . .'

It would be hard to find a single adjective to describe Cecil Provender. 'Spinsterly' would, in many ways, be suitable, but in one, perhaps most important, respect he differed from the majority of spinsters. On the other hand he was far too vinegary, for all his generosity and protectiveness, to deserve to be called 'motherly'. He was plump and bald, with a sad little mouth that always drooped sideways except when he gave his surprisingly bass laugh, ears that stuck out on either side of his pear-shaped face, and small eyes that glinted with something of the shrewd cunning of the Yorkshire father who had made his fortune for him. Unlike most people of his wealth and tastes, he dressed badly in clothes which, he told one with pride: 'I had made by my little man in Empoli. It's worth making the journey from Florence. He's so cheap—and so good.'

'Who is this Grecos?' I whispered, when the story of the 'distraction' had come to its close.

'Theo Grecos! But you must have heard about Theo Grecos—Madame la Maréchale? Surely you have?'

'No.'

'What have you been doing? With the possible exception of the Colossus of Maroussi he's the best-known figure in Athens.'

'I rarely go to Athens.'

'Yes, you seem to be fated to be provincial . . . Oh, dear, the spit from this horrible old man has begun to drip on the floor.' Cecil edged yet closer to me. 'Well, Theo . . . what shall I tell you about him? First, he was a great Air Ace—in one of those Balkan wars, against Bulgaria, or Yugoslavia, was it? Anyway he was the first—or one of the first men to fly an aeroplane in war. Then he's a composer. And a writer. And a dress designer. And a . . .'

But at this point I could no more hear what he whispered, for some soldiers were marching past the

9

schoolroom and as they marched they sang, after the fashion of Greek soldiers. I suppose there is no nation which loves music more and yet is more unmusical, and these country youths—I remembered now that Langada was a centre for the training of recruits—were bawling out their song in the most hideous dissonance, as they passed by the windows. They looked squat and grubby, their faces streaked by the rain and dust, and their boots dragging and stumbling; and yet as their raw voices reverberated about us, there was something jolly about them, I thought, something invincible and true. 'Cauchemar!' Cecil said. He had put his fingers to his ears.

For a while the lecturer attempted to speak against the noise outside; then he gave up. I was sorry, for there had been something oddly moving in the imposition of the one sound on the other—the single, civilised voice quoting Vergil (*'Orpheaque in medio posuit, silvasque sequentes . . .'*) with the artistry of an actor, while those many, crude voices outside yelled out their rhythmical chant to the clatter of boots on cobbles. Theo Grecos stood, legs wide apart and his lean hands on his hips, and waited, not with impatience or exasperation, but a kind of dreamy pleasure. His head was slightly on one side, as he too looked out of the window, and his mouth had formed itself into a gentle half-smile. Slowly, slowly the young voices faded across the marshes . . .

When the lecture at last ended Cecil said: 'Come and meet Theo.'

'I should like to.'

'At any rate *he's* enjoying himself.' A large crowd had gathered about the old man as he began to climb from the platform. 'Now I believe we have to go and watch a calf being slaughtered. I'm not awfully good at blood. I think I shall go and sleep in the car.' But I knew both that Cecil would be at the sacrifice and that he would manage to get himself the best place. He was a person of the liveliest curiosity, even though he liked to give the impression that little in life either pleased him or interested him. 'Ah, Theo! If we're going to this sacrifice, oughtn't we to go now? There are sure to be enormous crowds.'

'Now don't fuss. Everything has been arranged.' The old man tightened the knot of his scarf, as he looked at me with his pale green eyes. 'A compatriot of yours, Cecil?'

'Oh yes—I'm sorry. This is Frank Cauldwell. We were both up at Balliol.'

'Not at the same time surely?'

The question sounded innocent; but now, as I look back, I am certain that its intention was malicious: Cecil was sensitive about looking older than his years.

'Yes, at the same time.'

'Have you been long in Greece?'

'Two years.'

'Then why have I never met you? I know every Englishman who ever visits Greece. Why has no one mentioned you to me?' He spoke querulously, as though there had been a conspiracy to keep me away from him. 'Never mind.' He put a hand on my shoulder and looked down at me with his gentle half-smile. 'I am delighted to meet you, sir.'

'Come along, Theo!' Cecil cried impatiently.

'But I've told you—everything is arranged. There's no hurry at all.'

'Oh, I know your arrangements,' Cecil retorted rudely, in the tone I had so often heard him use to distracted officials from Cook's or American Express.

'Cecil is so impatient, isn't he?' the old man said in a mild tone: but I noticed that the gruyère cheese of his cheeks had flushed into two bright red spots.

In fact, Theo had made no arrangements and when we reached the courtyard we found it surrounded by dusty charabancs and lorries from which an impenetrable crowd of trippers from Salonica were pouring to view the spectacle. 'As I expected,' Cecil said grimly, when Theo had twice been told not to push by a woman with a solemn and shrivelled-looking child in her arms. 'We shall never get through.'

'I am afraid the Greeks are not very courteous on such occasions. But please wait a moment.'

Theo went over to a police officer whom I assumed to be of high rank both from the number of medals on his uniform and from his complete apathy at the spectacle of so many screaming, milling people. 'Good morning, sir,' I heard Theo say in Greek. He then introduced himself: 'Colonel Grecos, late of the Royal Greek Air Force', and explained that it was he who had both been lecturing on the Anastanarides at the village school and had written an article on them in *Kathimerini*.

'Ah,' said the police officer with a sour smile, 'so it is you we have to thank for all these crowds.' He glanced

12

for a moment at the woman with whom Theo had had his altercation; she had been pushed on to her hands and knees and her child was squealing beneath her. 'You and the Bishop,' he said.

Unperturbed Theo went on to explain I was a correspondent from the London *Times* and *Life* magazine, and that Cecil was a member of the British Parliamentary Delegation then visiting Greece. For good measure he added that General Stavrides, the Chief of Police, had told us to rely on his force at any time of need.

Our officer looked peevish; but he clapped his small, dimpled hands together and explained to two gendarmes that we were to be escorted to the front. 'Quite simple,' Theo said, evidently not realising that I could speak Greek. 'I had only to mention my name and these excellent fellows were put at our disposal.'

A way had been cleared for us, not without noisy resistance from our fellow spectators, to what looked like an ordinary kitchen table laid with nothing but circular loaves of bread, stamped with wheat-sheaves. Everyone was staring either at the loaves of bread or at each other, since there was nothing else to do. I found myself standing next to the blond foreigner. Theo kept glancing at him over my head and at last he said in a loud voice: 'These crowds are really *furchtbar*.' But the German still continued to glower morosely at the loaf of bread before him, gnawing at his nails as he did so. Theo hissed in my ear: 'Qui est ce garçon-là?'

'I don't know,' I said in Greek.

'Sembra molto interessante.'

'Theo, please tell this *hag* behind me not to swing on

the strap of my camera,' Cecil put in crossly. The 'hag' looked like a girl of seventeen or eighteen.

All at once we heard a rhythmical thud of drums and squeal of pipes, accompanied by a tinkle and clatter from a tambourine, as everyone began saying: 'They're coming! They're coming!'

'Theo, for heaven's sake, she's going to break this——'

'Oh, do be quiet!'

Slowly the Anastanarides pushed their way through the crowd: first an old man with the face of a sleepy pig, who danced as he shook an ikon from side to side over his head; then a boy with a drum, who hopped, crouching, from one leg to another as though he were playing hop-scotch; then an old woman, also brandishing an ikon, whose dance was a kind of rhythmic shuffle and glide; then a plump, girlish youth, vaguely self-conscious as he blew on a clarinet; and finally a jumble of people who capered, jogged and shook their hips with a trance-like kind of solemnity. 'The Orphic Rose!' Theo hissed. 'Look at the Orphic Rose!' Pinned to the ikon held aloft in the hands of the first old man was a faded pink artificial rose that looked as if it might have been cut off some old evening dress. As the Anastanarides continued to circle the table before us, I was aware that the German's whole vast body was shaking in time to their music; he was even clicking his fingers and his tongue.

'Theo, I told you that she would go and break this strap. . . . You stupid woman! Look what you've done!'

Two boys now appeared, one tugging at a calf by its tether while the other pushed from behind. They were enjoying this, and instead of having the blankly somnolent expression of the other Anastanarides, their skinny faces under their over-large caps were contorted with laughter. From time to time the boy behind would twist the animal's tail, as though it were the starter of a car, and it would leap into the air, while the whole crowd roared its amusement. Slowly this calf was led to the table, and innumerable hands held it down while the man with the sleepy pig-face brandished his ikon (smoke had so obscured its surface that it was impossible to see what it represented) before the animal's terrified eyes. He was muttering something unintelligible as he swayed from side to side, and it seemed to me then, though it may have been imagination, that in doing so he induced in the wretched creature a state of hypnosis. Certainly it hardly moved when he took two lighted candles which an old woman handed him, and stuck one in each of its ears; when he cut off a lock of hair from its forehead and burned it at a third candle; or when he made the sign of the cross over it with a sprinkling of holy water. There was a silence now except for his hoarsely muttering voice; the dancers were still.

'Quick!' said Theo. 'Get over to that pit over there. That's where they'll make the sacrifice. Where's Cecil?'

But Cecil, as I had expected, was already at the pit. No one had told him that the sacrifice would be there, but he had known it by the same unerring instinct that always told him where to find a seat in a crowded train.

Once again the German was beside me; and once again he stared away with that same brooding sullenness, this time at the straw with which the pit had been filled, while Theo murmured to me in German for his benefit:

15

'Ich weiss nicht, was soll es bedeuten,
Dass ich so traurig bin . . .'

I could not see the relevance of the quotation, but perhaps these were the only words of German that Theo knew.

'I hope I shan't faint,' Cecil said. He was busily adjusting the stops of his Leica; he had never looked better.

I, too, am not 'good at blood', and my memory of the actual sacrifice is blurred even as the faces of the eager spectators opposite me were blurred when I gazed across at them, with a nauseous buzzing in my ears, after the animal had slowly folded itself up on to its bed of wet straw. I have a recollection of the large freckled hand of the old man swinging a knife as he gazed skywards, his tawny eyelashes flickering over his pale blue, watery eyes as he murmured an invocation; I can hear again the curious tinkling noise, as of falling coins, when the blood first began to trickle into the basin held by one of the two boys who had brought the calf in; and I can remember, most clearly of all, the extraordinary long-drawn 'Ah-h-h!' from the whole crowd as the knife had plunged deep. To me it was a messy and savage end to what had been a ceremony so far beautiful in its simplicity; there is a cruelty in the Greeks which can be found in no other European nation except perhaps the Spanish. But when, afterwards, I told Theo this, he said loftily: 'Ah, I see that for all your two years in this country, you still have not learned really to appreciate us.'

The faces before me were still advancing and receding on wave after wave of nausea when I felt myself being pushed violently to one side. It was Götz Joachim who was butting, rather than thrusting, his way through the crowd, his head lowered while his hands flung people to one side or the other. He had reached a tree, and he leaned against it, his pink hair glinting in the sunlight.

'He is going to vomit,' Theo said. 'Poor boy.'

Having been told that the actual firewalking would not take place until the afternoon, we decided to have lunch and the driver of the hired car in which Theo and Cecil had travelled from Salonica to Langada began to carry innumerable cardboard boxes, paper bags and tins into the taverna where we had already seated ourselves. There were some young lieutenants from the Camp devouring plates of roast lamb that was probably roast goat, and they all gazed at us with a kind of solemn astonishment as Cecil unpacked one delicacy after another: brique and foie gras sandwiches, Scotch eggs, cold chicken and ham, russian salad, chocolate mousse, and Alpine strawberries and cream. 'You'd think they'd never seen any food in their lives,' Cecil grunted. 'What manners!' But then, in one of his unaccountable fits of generosity, he passed over to them a whole carton of sandwiches with nothing but a shrug and his small, bitter smile. In return we were sent a carafe of Naoussa wine, excellent in its raw astringency, which Cecil sipped and then proclaimed to be: 'Vinegar, my dear—just vinegar.'

Theo was fond of food: and when, later, I discovered how poor he was, I understood better his mounting excitement as each new delicacy was revealed and laid on the table before him. He kept smiling and rubbing his lean hands together between his knees as he murmured:

'Foie gras, foie gras! . . . Chicken! . . . Mousse! . . . Petits fours! . . . A meal for Lucullus! . . . You have done us proud, Cecil! You have really done us proud!' He ate in silence and must have consumed more than Cecil and I together.

Suddenly, as he was wiping the remainder of the russian salad off his plate with a piece of bread on the end of a fork, he looked up and said: 'There he is again. Now who do you think he is?'

We followed his gaze out through the door of the taverna into the square where the German was stooping over a tap, apparently brushing his teeth with the fore-finger of his right hand while with his left he clutched to himself some kind of painted pot. He had rolled his blue jeans up to his knees to reveal a pair of legs that had a curiously peeled, white appearance until they terminated in the grubbiness of his ankles. 'He's obviously German,' Theo said. 'But why have I never seen him before?'

'You ought to be thankful that you haven't,' Cecil replied.

'He must be quite six foot six.' Theo stretched an arm ac ross the table: 'These Scotch eggs are delicious.'

The German had begun to shamble over the baked ruts of the square, muttering to himself with lowered head, while his right hand beat a tattoo on the pot held in his left.

'He's coming in here,' Theo said.

Again the young officers all looked up, as the extra-ordinary tousled figure stood in the doorway, blinking in through the murk. The pot, I now saw, was shaped as a rotund evzone with *Langada* painted in yellow letters across the swelling belly. Theo had also noticed this, and he whispered to me. 'Where do you think he got the pot? I've been trying to get one of those for years.'

The German had passed by us into a corner of the taverna when his head hit one of the phallus-like rolls of a heavily seasoned dry tongue much eaten in Macedonia, that were hanging from the ceiling. The roll, unhooked at the impact, began to fall and, instinctively, the German put up both hands to catch it, forgetting the pot which crashed to the floor and was at once shattered to pieces. One of the lieutenants gave a high-pitched squeal of delight, while the others all smiled down at the table. The German was kneeling on the floor picking up the broken shards, which he dusted in turn on the sleeve of his tartan wind-jacket. When they had all been collected he carried them over to his table and, sitting down, began to fit them against one another; but since he had no glue, this seemed to me a futile exercise—as he himself must have at last realised, for all at once he pushed the pieces from him, with the petulant and humiliated expression of a child who has smashed a toy, and called for the waiter, from whom I heard him order a plate of bean soup. As he waited for his food to be brought to him, he rummaged in his several pockets to produce odd tattered five-hundred and thousand drachmae notes which he smoothed out, counted and then placed in a heap before him.

Theo had been watching him intently and now he leant forward: 'Excuse me, sir.' The German continued to smooth out a crumpled note. 'Excuse me, sir,' Theo said louder.

The German looked up, his harelip seeming to twitch in apprehension.

'Do you speak English?' Theo pursued.

'A little.' The voice was of a rumbling profundity, as though vast express trains were racing deep in the bowels of the earth.

'Ah, good. I was wondering if you could tell me where you bought that pot which has just had such an unfortunate—er—accident.'

The German explained that there was a small shop on the outskirts of the town, and agreed that he would lead Theo there if the old man wished. Meanwhile the waiter had put down before the German a steaming plate of dried beans cooked in oil and garlic and raising his spoon with a murmured 'Excuse me' he began to gulp noisily. '*Appetit!*' said Theo and turned to hiss at Cecil:

'May I ask him over?'

Cecil pulled a face, as though he had just put something bitter in his mouth. 'Must you?' he said.

The German was asking the price of a glass of wine as Theo pleaded: 'He can't afford anything but that plate of soup. And we shall never eat all this.' He pointed to the feast before us.

'You're making a good try,' Cecil said. 'Oh, all right, all right.'

Theo got up and made a ceremonious bow at the other table as he said: 'Forgive me for troubling you once again, sir, but my friends and I would be extremely honoured if you would come and join us.'

The pink eyelashes blinked uncomprehendingly and the large Adam's apple bounced up and down as the German swallowed his mouthful of soup.

'Do please join us.' Theo pointed in our direction with the palm of one hand.

The German began to pick up what lay on the table before him: first the tattered and soiled scraps of money which he stuffed into a pocket; then the broken shards which he proceeded to tie up in a filthy khaki handkerchief; and finally the plate of soup. Then he came over.

'Do you really want to eat that mess?' Cecil said, nodding at the soup-plate. 'We've so much food here.'

'Yes, I shall eat it,' the German said stolidly. He put the plate down, and extended a paw: 'Götz Joachim,' he said. 'Götz Joachim . . . Götz Joachim.' We each of us winced in turn and surreptitiously rubbed our bruised fingers under the table.

'And what has brought you here?' Theo asked.

'The firewalking.' Noisily the soup was sucked from the spoon down the bull-like throat.

'I mean—what has brought you to Greece?'

Götz Joachim smiled: it was the first time I had seen him do so, and it was the first time that I found myself looking closely at him without a feeling of horror. It says much for the charm of that smile that it could work this transfiguration. 'I love Greece,' he said simply.

'Bravo!' Theo put an arm round one of the German's massive, slumped shoulders. 'That is the best reason in the world for being in Greece. . . . Now you must eat this Scotch egg. Do you have Scotch eggs in Germany?'

'I don't think Frank has had an egg, has he?' Cecil put in. The egg was the last, Theo himself having already devoured four.

21

'It's quite all right,' I said embarrassed. 'I don't really want it.'

'Come—you must be hungry,' Theo said to Götz, making no acknowledgement of my act of self-sacrifice.

The egg went in two large bites, and Theo, who had watched in admiration, now began to pile slice after slice of chicken and ham on a plate. 'How's that?' he asked.

'Vonderful!' It was, I later discovered, one of the two words that Götz always used when he felt either pleasure or admiration: the other was 'fantastic'.

Theo continued to question him: but though, being a Greek, he had no inhibitions about probing into the most intimate details of the lives of strangers, he could get little from Götz. The German was unmarried, and he came from Munich where his father was 'in business'; he was twenty-eight years old; and he had been travelling about Greece for the last two and a half years. He was a photographer, he added.

'Then where is your camera?' Theo asked.

Götz explained simply that his camera was in pawn.

'Then how can you make any money?'

The German shrugged his shoulders and began to laugh uproariously at the expression of concern on Theo's face. Soon the two men began to laugh together, Theo's arm once again about Götz's shoulder as they rocked to and fro. I guessed that they had both drunk too much of the 'just vinegar' which the officers had sent us.

' "... The loud laugh that spoke the vacant mind," ' Cecil murmured.

After lunch, Götz went back to rejoin the Anastanarides in their smoky shack, Cecil settled himself to sleep in the car, and Theo announced that he was going across the marshes to search for a species of willow only to be found in this part of Macedonia. 'Don't be late,' Cecil said. He turned to me: 'Theo has no sense of time. We missed the 'plane when we came from Athens, and had to wait a whole day. . . . What time will the firewalking begin?'

'My friend, the Commissioner of Police, says not till after four. He has, of course, got seats for us. Good seats.'

'Well, be back at three-thirty.'

It was not until half-past four that Theo trudged, dusty but cheerful, into the café where I was sitting reading a book. 'Look!' he cried triumphantly, holding out what, to my inexperienced eyes, seemed to be nothing but a handful of tattered branches. 'I've found it. Do you see how the leaves grow? The abnormality lies in the——'

'It's already half-past four. Don't you think we ought to be going?'

'Does botany not interest you?' he asked coldly.

'No, not really. But anyway, we must get to the fire-walking——'

Theo rearranged the branches in his hand, shaking them so that their dust left a film on my half-drunk cup of coffee. 'It must be strange to have lived all one's life in towns.'

I had never said that I had lived all my life in towns; it was not even true. But now I merely continued: 'Cecil will be cross, if we don't wake him at once.'

'Yes, yes,' Theo said. 'You're quite right, quite right.'

His feelings towards Cecil were a curious mixture of affection, fear and that resentment which we involuntarily bear towards those from whom we are forced to accept charity. 'Cecil is not very—patient,' he added.

So far from being patient, Cecil was in the vilest of tempers when he awoke. I knew just how he would be feeling as Theo shook his shoulder. There would be pins and needles in one of his legs and the other would seem to be three inches shorter than when he had gone to sleep. The skin of his face would feel too tight, his tongue too loose, and his throat too small. As he moved to get himself out of the car a small stone would seem to rattle about in his head while a large one would shift uneasily in his stomach. 'Oh God!' he muttered. Then he hiccoughed and said: 'That foul wine! . . . What time is it?'

'It's past four,' Theo said evasively.

Cecil looked at the gold watch on his thin, hairy wrist. 'Past four! Do you realise that it's now nearly five. And I particularly told you—oh really, Theo! I expect we've missed everything.' His tie had slipped down and Theo, tucking his branches under his arm, put out two hands to adjust the knot as he murmured soothingly, 'Now, don't worry. Don't worry. The Commissioner of Police——'

'You'll dirty my tie—look at your fingers! And what are you doing with those branches? . . . Oh come on, come on!' He strode off, hobbling a little on his left leg, and we hurried after him. 'There, I told you so!' he turned and hissed at us as, in the distance, we could see a vast throng milling about the enclosure in which the fire-walking would take place. 'What did I tell you?'

There then followed some ten minutes during which Theo ran from group to group of police officers, explaining who we were (I had, by then, become Sir Winston Churchill's son-in-law and Cecil was the Argentine ambassador) while Cecil shrilled in English at the gendarmes who were holding the crowds back from the entrance to the already packed enclosure: 'What does this mean?' he demanded of them. 'Why can't we go in? Do you realise that I've come all the way from Italy just to see this? I've never come across such idiotic inefficiency!' He turned to me: 'Shall I slip them something?'

'Would it be wise? Don't forget that the British now have a Police Mission in Greece.'

'Then it's a pity that they didn't give their advice on how to organise this show.'

Theo eventually arrived with the calming assurance that 'everything was arranged'. 'The moment they knew that I was Colonel Grecos of the historic Florina incident, all went smoothly.'

'It seemed to take them a long time to find out,' Cecil said venomously.

'Oh, naturally, all the young officers wanted to have a word with me.'

Once again escorted by two gendarmes through the protesting crowds, we found ourselves in the second row of chairs that had been arranged for Government officials, the Corps Diplomatique and friends of the Mayor. 'So,' said Theo, sighing as he attempted to ease his chair backwards on to the knees of the matron seated behind him, and at the same time thrust his long legs forward, 'it's not too bad, is it? We shall see splendidly. . . . Excuse me, sir!' He had succeeded in all but tipping the occupant of the chair in front—an E.C.A. administrator—into the dust. 'All's well that ends well—isn't that what you say?'

But all was far from ending well. Two old men had pushed a cart containing dry branches into the enclosure and had built up a fire; and now, as we waited, the dry wind blowing the smoke into our faces so that our throats tickled and our eyes streamed, I noticed that, time and time again, the crowds succeeded in breaking through the cordons of policemen. At first these intruders contented themselves with either joining the mob already packed behind our seats or filling the gangways; but then, when these places had all been wedged so tight that they could no longer stand there, they began to thrust themselves between us and the bonfire on which the Anastanarides would dance. The police tried to push them away; but they would retreat momentarily only to surge back again until the whole narrow space about the smoking bonfire was full of shoving, screaming, coughing people. I saw a policeman pursuing a small girl, rather as though they were playing a game of hide-and-seek among the crowds until catching her he passed her out over the barbed wire of the enclosure; another policeman put both arms round a struggling old woman and lugged her to the entrance where she was unceremoniously expelled with a push on the behind. The Chief of Police to whom Theo had originally spoken now began to stride up and down, all his former apathy gone as he shouted at the people before us: 'I command you—

please leave this place! Leave this place! Leave this place!'
The crowds continued to fight their way in. 'I appeal to
you, as Greeks. Think of these foreign diplomats—' as
he pointed at our rows of chairs, I thought that really
Cecil had made a convincing Argentine ambassador—
'who have come here to view this spectacle. We have
here a reporter from the London *Times*! A reporter from
Life magazine! What will they write about the discipline
and order in Greece?' I felt a vague schizophrenia at this
splitting of my personality. Then he threatened: 'If you
do not move, the Anastanarides will not dance! They
will not dance! I shall not allow them to dance! I warn
you! Unless you move, nothing will happen!' There
were guffaws, obscene shouts and a gentle patter of stones.
Tearfully now the Chief of Police demanded: 'What
am I to do? What am I to say to you? I am ashamed of
you! I am ashamed of myself. I am ashamed of Greece!'

'We shall see nothing,' Cecil said. 'Oh, damn them!
What are the police doing?' He stood up and shouted:
'Get out of the way! How do you expect us to see? You've
no right to be there! You!' He pointed at the Chief of
Police. 'Do something about this.'

Theo caught him by the back of his coat and pulled
him on to his chair. 'Don't be silly, Cecil. You'll gain
nothing like that.' Another gust of smoke swept over us
and we all began coughing. 'Have you noticed how
catching hysteria always is?' Theo murmured to me. He
pointed to the American administrator who was poking
a Greek peasant with his walking-stick and shouting at
the same time in English: 'You heard me! Get to hell out
of here! Get to hell out of here! Beat it!'

Far off there now sounded the thud of drums, the squeal of pipes. A momentary hush fell, as everyone listened: the dancers were coming. Then, with an even more frenzied shouting, those outside the enclosure resumed the struggle to fight their way in, while those within no less tenaciously struggled to retain or improve their places. 'Sit down! Sit down!' the crowds behind us shouted at the people standing between our chairs and the bonfire. 'Sit down! We can see nothing!' Stones skimmed over our heads as the two parties entered into battle. I saw a boy with a jaggedly bleeding cut over one temple gleefully lob stone after stone into the crowded pit behind us; an old man was having hysterics; a child was screaming as it was pushed nearer and nearer the flames.

No doubt many people would have been injured if, at that moment, the Anastanarides had not appeared. I myself could see nothing from where I sat except the ikons bobbing above the crowds, as the music drew closer; but suddenly Theo grabbed my arm and shouted: 'Look who is with them!'

'Who?' But even as I said the word, I had a glimpse, momentarily, of sunlight flashing on straw-coloured hair. 'The German!' I exclaimed.

'The German!' Theo echoed. 'But what has happened to Cecil?' Cecil's chair was empty; and before I could look for him, the man seated behind me began to climb over the back of my chair into my lap. He was a large man, in a dark blue suit, and I guessed that he was probably a haberdasher. His expression was bemusedly intent and, as he was no acrobat, he had to assist himself by clutching to my collar while his small feet, in their shiny, pointed black shoes, scrabbled on the wooden back of the chair. 'What are you doing?' I asked in Greek.

He grunted, but said nothing.

'Please leave go—both of me and the chair.'

He toppled and steadied himself by clutching my ear.

'Get down!' I shouted. I gave him a push and he slipped across the lap of the matron beside him. At once he jumped up and hissed at me: 'You are very nervy.' Again he began to scrabble up my seat, this time clutching me by the hair while his toes sought for footholds in my pockets. Again I tried to push him, but he only clutched tighter. At this point Theo saw what was happening, and turning, he lashed out at the man with his branches of willow; leaves and dust descending upon me as the man gave a roar of mingled anger and pain. Again he fell into the lap of the matron, and again he leapt up, this time to grapple with Theo. But somehow, not intentionally, I got between the two. Fortunately my assailant was an even less expert fighter than myself, and we merely swayed from side to side, our arms on each other's shoulders, until innumerable hands plucked us apart.

'He is a foreigner,' the matron shouted, and the people about us took up her cry: 'A foreigner! Fancy attacking a foreigner! What will he think of Langada? What will he think of Greece?'

All at once I felt a desire to get away: shouting at my assailant, 'Thank you for your philoxeny!' (I transliterate the word since the English 'hospitality' does not make an adequate translation), I began to fight for the entrance. By then I was in a panic and I know that I behaved badly:

I swore in Greek and English, pushed, pulled, and even, on one occasion, punched a man in the stomach when he refused to give way. Suddenly I slipped, my toe catching a chair, and I was down with the crowd over me. I struggled to rise, but felt a boot graze my cheek; again I struggled and this time something jolted in my right ribs with an agonising impact. I tried to protect my face with my arms.

Someone was shouting above me; I felt two vast hands under my arm-pits. I was being dragged along, my heels tearing at the soil; I was half-crying with fear and exasperation. 'There!' I had been dumped on a slope beside some scraps of soiled paper, rusty tin-cans and a goat which jerked away on its tether, leaping into the air, as I and my rescuer neared it. I put my hands to my face and found that it was wet.

'Blood!' a deep voice said, followed by a rumble of laughter.

I looked up. Legs wide apart and hands on hips, there stood before me a gendarme who looked as if he might be heavy-weight boxing champion of the Greek police force. He had a moustache so large that one could see little of his face beyond two brilliant, jet-coloured eyes, a massive chin of the purple colour common among men who have to shave twice a day, and a nose that had obviously been flattened by someone's fist. He was the exact antithesis of Götz, since his size and almost brutal ugliness, so far from repelling, exerted a kind of fascination. He now stooped above me, and examined my cut eye with fingers that were certainly clumsy and probably not clean. He whistled in a way that alarmed me, and then said: 'Come!' Putting an arm round my shoulder he began to support me up a track that led to the central square. 'We shall go to the chemist.'

'But you'll miss the firewalking,' I said.

'It doesn't matter.'

'Have you seen it before?'

'No.'

'Then you're not from here?'

'From here!' He gave his rumbling laugh as though I had asked some absurd question. 'I'm from Crete. Have you been to Crete?'

'No.' I now had some difficulty in talking, as I attempted to staunch my blood with a handkerchief.

'In the war I had a good English friend in Crete.'

I guessed at once who it would be and mentioned the name.

The gendarme thumped me on the back, delighted. 'You know him?' he asked.

'A little.'

'I helped him capture the German General.'

I had so often been told this by Cretans that I was beginning to think that the whole island had taken part in this operation, to a man. 'Oh, yes,' I said with no particular surprise or enthusiasm; and no doubt it was the apathy that goaded my rescuer into telling me the story of how he had, single-handed, cut off the head of a drunken German. I must have shown my squeamishness, for he again thumped me between the shoulder-blades, giving his bass roar of laughter, as he shouted in reassurance: 'The English and the Cretans—friends, always friends!'

31

Theo arrived at the chemist's shop, just as the little man in a grubby off-white coat had pressed some sticking plaster on to my cheek and turned to the gendarme to say jovially: 'Now you can take him away and post him.'

'Ah, there you are!' Theo still had his willow branches in his hand, but almost all the leaves had been shed. 'Everyone is looking for you—I have just had a word with the Chief of Police and he was about to send out some motor-cyclists.' Theo, like most of his countrymen, had a passion for dramatising even the most trivial happenings. 'We were quite distracted. I saw you make off after that unpleasant incident, and I even saw you fall. But of course I couldn't get to you, try as I might. Are you badly hurt?'

'No, just bruised ribs and a cut cheek, thank you.'

'No stitches?'

I shook my head.

'Nothing broken?'

'Oh, good heavens, no.' I began to wish I could produce at least a sprain in order to satisfy him.

'Shock, I expect. It must have been an ordeal.'

'I daresay I'd have fared worse if it hadn't been for my friend here.'

Theo had already been glancing at the gendarme, and now he made a dignified bow as he pronounced: 'My friend and I are extremely grateful to you. I shall mention your conduct to General Stavrides when I lunch with him tomorrow. What is your name?'

'Kyrmizakis, sir.'

'Ah, a Cretan, I see.'

'Yes, sir.'

'Splendid fellows, these Cretans,' he turned to me, in English. 'It's the Berber strain.'

'Did you see the firewalking?'

'See—nothing! But . . . I felt it. That is the important thing. I felt it. All that shouting and agitated movement and heedless pressing onwards, as the divine wind blew through them! It was magnificent. . . . I doubt if you see anything like that in your over-civilised England.'

I repressed the desire to mention Wembley, and asked: 'And Cecil! How did he fare?'

'He saw everything—every single thing!'

'Of course.'

'Of course!' Theo chuckled, his pointed chin sinking deep into the folds of his scarf. 'But the poor German boy—Cecil tells me that he jumped on to the fire and then had to jump off pretty quick.'

As Theo said this, the bell over the door of the shop tinkled and Götz himself limped in. His face was blackened with smoke, his eyes were red-rimmed. In one hand he carried his brown canvas gym-shoes and in the other he trailed a pair of soggy, khaki socks. He came towards us, performing the difficult feat of walking on his heels, and gave an embarrassed smile. 'I was not much good at it,' he said.

'Burned?' Theo asked.

'Yes.' Götz sank on to a chair, and raising one vast foot between both hands, peered down at it.

'Badly?'

'Blisters everywhere.'

Theo and the gendarme were now also peering at the

33

foot and I realised that I had completely forfeited both their attention and their sympathy. Cecil came in:

'Oh, here you are,' he said casually. 'You were a fool, you missed everything. It really does happen, you know. There was one old girl who was fairly leaping about on the flames, and the extraordinary thing is that even though her skirt reached to the ground it was not even singed. I've just been examining it. . . . I got some excellent photographs—a really funny one of our German at the moment when he——' I put out a warning hand. 'What's the matter? . . . Oh, I see.' Cecil strolled over to the group fussing around Götz. He looked with extreme distaste at the grubby and blistered foot, and then turned away as he said: 'In life nowadays there's no place for the amateur. . . . Who's the friend?'

'Which friend?'

'The policeman.'

I explained how I had been rescued. 'What fun!' Cecil said, in the toneless voice which he used both when he felt no interest and when he wished to conceal his interest.

After Götz's feet had been bandaged up, we all went into a taverna to drink some ouzo. The gendarme, having swallowed four or five glasses in rapid succession, once again began to guffaw and thump me between the shoulder-blades as he resumed the blood-curdling narrative of his exploits against the Germans. Holding out his massive hairy hands he demonstrated how he had strangled a man who had violated one of his cousins; then he tossed back some more of the fiery, opalescent spirit. Cecil began to whisper in Theo's ear.

Theo turned to me. 'You will of course come back in our car with us? We can arrange for your bicycle to be brought in by a lorry—perhaps we can even strap it on the car. . . . And you, Herr Joachim—how are you planning to return to Salonica?'

'I think hitch-hike.'

'With your feet in that condition? . . . No, you had far better come with us.' I suddenly received a sharp kick on the ankle which, I suspect, Cecil had intended for Theo. 'We have a large car, with plenty of room.' Now Theo turned to the gendarme and asked in Greek: 'And how do you return?'

'There's a lorry for us, leaving at seven.'

'Can we give you a lift—if you don't want to wait about, that is? You were so kind to our friend here.' He indicated me. 'Have you more duty this evening?'

The gendarme shook his head.

'Ah. Good.'

The car was an American one and as the driver opened the back door, Theo said: 'Will you get in, Herr Joachim? Then I shall place myself between you and Mr Cauldwell. ... Our host and the excellent Kyrmizakis can sit in front. All right?'

As we began to race back to Salonica through the gathering twilight, Theo put one bony hand on Götz's knee and another on mine: 'Well, this seems a most satisfactory end to a day of alarms and excursions. . . . Eh, Cecil?'

'Most satisfactory, Theo.'

THE next day Cecil asked me to join him and Theo on
an expedition to Michaniona, a small fishing village some
twelve miles from Salonica. 'People tell me that it's *fruit-
ful*,' he explained. Wherever he travelled, Cecil always
had such tips about places; and nearly always such tips
proved reliable. I had often wondered how he came by
them.

When I arrived, five minutes late, outside the cinema
where we had arranged to meet, Cecil alone was there.
'Theo has disappeared,' he greeted me, without even
answering my 'Good morning'.

'Disappeared?' I was alarmed by the dramatic announcement.

'A moment ago he was looking at these photographs'
—he pointed to some cinema stills of Alan Ladd's torso,
yellow and curling at the edges, fixed with drawing-
pins to a board by the door—'and then, when I looked
round for him, I couldn't find him anywhere. He's
maddening, absolutely maddening. It's been like
this the whole trip. If he disappeared for good I wouldn't
mind so much, but of course I can always be certain
that he'll pop back for the next meal. He hasn't got a
penny.'

Even at such moments I had the impression, when I was talking to Cecil, that he was giving me only half his attention. He was exasperated with Theo, that of course was plain; yet as he grumbled about him to me, I became aware that his gaze was moving away over my shoulder and that his voice had taken on the mechanical tone with which one repeats a well-learned lesson while thinking of something else. It was rarely that one felt one was in complete contact with Cecil for more than five minutes at a stretch; he had the restlessness of a person waiting for a train that never comes, and his restlessness used to transmit itself to others so that when one stayed with him in his luxurious villa in Florence one found one-self switching the radiogram off and on, picking up and putting down a number of books which one never finished reading, and standing for long, vacant intervals on the balcony overlooking the Fiesole road as if in ex-pectation of a guest more amusing than those already gathered around one.

'Oh, there he is!' Theo was on the opposite side of the road, nervously stepping out into the gutter and then drawing back on to the pavement as, far off, a vehicle could be seen approaching. 'Theo!' Cecil shouted. 'Come here at once! Come here!'

At the sound of the imperious voice the old man looked right and left with a kind of fumbling panic, then lowered his head on which, I noticed, he was wearing a small green beret, and charged towards us, narrowly missing one of the mustard-coloured coffins on wheels which pass for trams in Salonica.

'Where have you been?' Cecil demanded.

37

'Good morning, Mr Cauldwell.' Theo bowed to me with ceremonious dignity.

'Where have you been?' Cecil repeated.

'I remembered that the Cosmopolite Hotel was just round that corner, so I thought I would go and see our friend,' Theo explained gently. 'He was in bed.'

'What friend?'

'Our German friend. You must really visit that hotel, Cecil—I'm sure you would find it—er—interesting. The poor boy was in a dormitory for six—at this hour the other occupants were not, of course, there. Such a curious collection of belongings,' he went on dreamily, 'all mixed up together: dirty socks, and a piano-accordion, and a soldier's belt and a copy of the *Reader's Digest*——'

'Oh, let's go!' Cecil put in rudely.

'But we'll have to wait for the German.'

'The German? Why should we wait for the German?'

'Well, he looked so pathetically lonely there in that narrow bed in that enormous cellar—and he said he had nothing to do and nowhere to go——'

'Oh, Theo, really! So I suppose you've asked him to join us?'

Theo nodded.

'No, really, Theo!'

'He won't keep us a moment. Fortunately he appeared to be in bed with all his clothes on, and he tells me that he only shaves once a week. . . . You don't mind, do you?' He now turned to me. 'I think he's a good sort.'

'Of course I don't mind.'

Götz now appeared, looking exactly as he had looked the previous day except that he was wearing sandals instead of the brown canvas gym-shoes and that his eyes seemed to be still half gummed together with sleep. He was carrying under one arm a bulging brown paper envelope stuffed with his photographs, which turned out to be of a quite unusual excellence when he showed them to us at lunch. 'Hello,' he said. 'Good morning.' Cecil did not reply but Theo said: 'Ah, but how quick you have been!'

Götz, who was now standing opposite me, replied with a massive yawn and stretch, not bothering to turn away or even to raise one of his paws to his gaping mouth. I was reminded of how on Sunday mornings in Greece one passes the open doors of the cinemas that are being 'aired' for the next week; the odour that escaped from the cavern of his mouth was not, at that moment, unlike the odour of that seven days' 'fug'.

'Have you found a taxi, Theo?' Cecil demanded.

'No, not yet. There's a rank in the square.'

Cecil made an exclamation of annoyance and shot off, pursued by Theo and then by Götz and myself, Götz still limping from his burns of the previous day.

In the square there followed an involved argument between Theo and Cecil which I had difficulty in understanding, since it was carried on almost entirely in mumbled asides and whispers; it seemed to be about the taxi we should choose, but as there was one large, comfortably modern Buick gleaming in the middle of the line of otherwise battered pre-war vehicles, I wondered how there could possibly be any dispute. Theo was going to one car after another, peering in and saying a few words to the driver; after which Cecil would also peer in, and they would again begin arguing. From time to time I would catch some fragment of what they whispered:

'. . . We'd better take that one there.'

'That one?'

'No, *that* one, you fool!'

'But he wants a hundred and fifty thousand. It's preposterous.'

'I've told you I don't care how much he wants.'

'I think the Citroen would be a better investment.'

'Which is the Citroen?'

'That one.'

'No, certainly not!'

A minute later I heard:

'. . . But where is he from?'

'Tripolis.'

'Ah, Tripolis. One can usually rely on Tripolis.'

'Only Patras is better.'

'And Heracleion.'

'What's his name?'

'Epaminondas.'

'What?'

'Epaminondas.'

'But I've never heard that name before! Tell him that we'll take him.'

I began to wonder whether we had been choosing a car or a driver; and for some reason, I all at once remembered the last time I had seen Cecil, when both of us were leaving England, he for his Florence villa and I for my job in Salonica. Since I was to travel as far as Florence as a passenger in his Jaguar, he had asked me to spend the night before our departure at his mother's country house near Folkestone. Lady Provender was a small, vital and sharp-tongued woman who, it was obvious, adored her only son and was adored in turn by him. When the time came to say goodbye Cecil embraced her with the words: 'It's sad that we should see so little of each other, Mother —you here, and I in Florence.'

'Yes, my dear, it is sad.' Lady Provender patted his hand which she held in both of hers. Then she looked up at him and smiled: 'But I'm quite sure that you did right when you decided to settle abroad.'

I was beginning to see now what she must have meant.

That morning Theo was wearing an extraordinary ring which covered almost the whole of his right forefinger. He had, he explained, made it himself from three sea-shells and it represented the Marriage of Heaven and Hell —a piece of symbolism which, I must confess, eluded me as much as the driver who had been the first to comment on it. On Theo's knobbly, wax-coloured finger the shells, of the same colour and texture as his skin, seemed to grow together like some monstrous excrescence. 'I make shell jewellery for Mrs Rhys, for the Queen, and for the wife of the British Ambassador,' Theo said com-placently. 'All my jewellery is, of course, fantasio-metric.' It was the first time I had heard this word; it was not to be the last.

'It's vonderful!' Götz exclaimed.

The young man, Epaminondas from Tripolis, who was driving the car, shrugged his well-padded shoulders and smiled superciliously as he said in Greek: 'I wouldn't give a cigarette for that ring.'

41

'No, I don't suppose you would,' Theo retorted coldly. 'I don't expect you to understand its significance.'

The young man laughed; he had a face that was 'fresh' in both senses of the word, the colour agreeably high and the expression disagreeably insolent. The nails of his little fingers were grown to mandarin-like lengths. 'There's no accounting for taste,' he now replied airily. 'I certainly wouldn't want to be seen with three sea-shells dangling from one finger.'

'This young man is extremely impertinent,' Theo said in English. 'The advantage of coming from Tripolis is usually outweighed by that disadvantage, I find: the people are all ill-bred.'

'I can understand English,' Epaminondas said in Greek. I did not believe him; but one usually realises when uncomplimentary things are being said about one in a language one does not know.

'Get on with your driving,' Theo said, 'and mind your own business.'

'What are you saying to him?' Cecil demanded. He turned to me: 'Theo always succeeds in rubbing up everyone the wrong way.'

Simultaneously the young man had said something to Theo which must have been unusually insulting as Theo went bright red and shouted: 'Get on with your driving and shut up! Shut up!'

'Theo, I forbid you to behave like that to the driver. What are you doing to the poor boy? Can't you leave him alone? What's the matter with you?'

'I will not be insulted,' Theo said doggedly. 'Not for anyone. Not even for you.'

There was silence until we reached Michaniona.

The proximity of this small fishing village had been for me one of the few consolations of living in a city which Edmond About seems to me aptly to have described as 'an ante-room to Hell'. At all seasons Michaniona was equally beautiful. In winter, I would take a 'bus out to it and would walk along the shore deserted except for a few solitary fishermen mending their boats; the air would be icy and clear, the sky and sea dizzying in their candour, there would be no sound but the lapping of waves, the screams of sea-birds, and, far off, the steady plock-plock-plock of an axe pruning olive trees. On a spring day such as this the beach-side tavernas and cafés, closed during the winter, would once more be open, though their owners would still be re-thatching with bamboo the concrete platforms on which the tables were set and re-painting, olive-green or red, the bathing-huts which looked like rows of narrow horse-boxes; a few people, usually American or English, would venture into the sea which they would screamingly proclaim to be 'freezing' although, already, it would be warmer than the sea in England in June. In summer, I would come here at night on the crowded, lurching steamer which had a loud-speaker so noisy that even when it was five miles from shore I could hear its music across the water from my flat. I would arrive sticky and dusty and cross, fling off my clothes and race into the moonlit waves, so charged with phosphorus that when one raised an arm the flesh glowed as if one had dipped it in luminous paint.

Even Cecil seemed to be delighted with the place. He took two or three photographs of the shore, receding

43

smooth and hard as though it were made of concrete, and then handed his camera to Götz: 'You're supposed to be good at this sort of thing, aren't you? Take me some pretty pictures.' I knew that Götz's photographs would be far better than any that Cecil took; and I guessed, perhaps uncharitably, that Cecil would later pass them off as his own. Cecil ordered some 'ouzo' and a plate of 'mezedes' —the tit-bits of cheese, fish or meat that are served with that drink—and then sank down into a deck-chair and crossed his plump thighs. 'It's rather agreeable here.' Theo and I sat down on either side of him. Then, with his usual restlessness, he jerked himself upright to ask: 'What's become of the driver?'

'He's inside the café.'

'Oh. . . . And what on earth is the German doing?'

The only two other customers were a pair of girls who lay side by side on deck-chairs, glistening like seals with the oil that they had spread on their dark brown bodies. Each was plumper and more hirsute than English taste would approve, but undeniably attractive. Their feet and dangling hands were curiously small, their breasts generous above their wide hips; their coarse black hair had been cropped close, their lips, finger-nails and toe-nails had all been painted the same pillar-box red. Each wore a cotton pad over her eyes as protection from the sun. Götz was creeping towards them over the sand, moving from a squatting position which made him look like some vast bird of prey; the Leica was raised to his eye.

Suddenly he clicked; then he went behind them and photographed them again, from above. Cecil shot up in

44

his chair: 'Ho!' he yelled, furious. 'What are you doing? Don't waste the film! Bring the camera here!'

The shout woke the two girls, and brought Götz shambling in embarrassment towards us.

'Just concentrate on the views,' Cecil said crossly. 'I don't want the human interest.'

Götz looked like a sulky boy, extending his lower lip and kicking with one toe at the sand as he said: 'They'll be wonderful photographs—you wait and see.'

'I've no doubt,' Cecil said drily. 'Now sit down and drink some ouzo.'

'Why has he brought us five glasses?' I queried naïvely. 'We're only four, aren't we?'

'I thought we'd ask our driver to eat with us. It seemed the friendly thing to do. I must say I like the absence of class distinctions in Greece.' I had never yet known Cecil to travel anything but first class whether abroad or in England. 'Theo, do go in and tell him that there's a glass of ouzo waiting.'

Götz rose: 'Shall I go in for you?'

'No, no, let Theo go.' Cecil smiled at me as the old man walked off, patient and stiff. 'Really that piece of *bijouterie* that Madame la Maréchale is sporting today! I entirely agree with our driver—he showed the most excellent taste.'

Theo now returned, shaking his head on its long, sinewy neck: 'He won't come.'

'What do you mean "he won't come"?'

'He says he prefers to eat by himself.'

'But didn't you tell him that we wanted him to——'

'Yes, of course I told him. But he says he won't come.'

45

Cecil stared blankly at the horizon, while the corners of his small, bitter mouth twisted in exasperation and then sagged downwards. He turned on Theo: 'This is your fault.'

'My fault?'

'If you hadn't been so rude to him—so needlessly rude to him——'

'He was rude to me.'

'He was only joking. If you wear an absurd ring like that, you must expect people to joke.'

'He was impertinent,' Theo said. 'I am sure our friends here will agree with me—he was thoroughly impertinent.' Götz and I both looked uncomfortable at being drawn into the quarrel.

'You're so touchy!' Cecil exclaimed. 'So anxious to preserve your dignity! And so tactless!'

I admired the way in which Theo controlled himself, and instead of retorting to these charges continued to place one tit-bit after another into his mouth with trembling hand. I knew already that while he was so far from his base he would not wish to risk any irrevocable break with Cecil; probably he did not even have enough money in his pocket to pay for a train ticket back. What I did not then know was that he had an affection for Cecil and a profound understanding of all his whims and vagaries which made him remember, as I always forgot, that the best way to deal with such outbursts of spleen was merely to ignore them.

Theo turned to Götz: 'Have you ever been to Tirnavos?'

'On Clean Monday, you mean?' Clean Monday is the last day before Lent in the Orthodox Calendar.

46

Theo was delighted: 'How do you know about Clean Monday at Tirnavos?' he asked.

Götz shrugged his shoulders, and gave the amiable grin that alone made it possible for one to look for long at his face. 'I have never been there. But I hear that it is *fantastic.*'

'Fantastic.' Theo echoed that characteristic word with satisfaction. 'You know, of course, that all the women are shut up for the night? The authorities are making an effort to stamp out the practices, but I fancy it will be many a long year before they succeed.'

'What is this? What are you talking about?' Cecil had ceased to stare moodily at the horizon and now swung round. 'Where is Tirnavos? What goes on there? What day, did you say?'

As Cecil's interest was won, so Götz's was lost: the two girls had risen from their chairs, and having tweaked their bathing-costumes into position, each now began to pull a rubber cap on her short wiry hair with an orientally languorous grace. Standing side by side, with their chubby, dimpled knees and arms, their generously sculptured navels and handsome, sloe-black eyes under arched brows, they might have been two Matisse odalisques: and Götz was watching them with a trance-like reverence that might even have flattered that master. He had a raised fork in one hand, with a sardine on the end of it, and the oil slipped off in glistening drops to join the other stains that covered his blue jeans.

'. . . the women have their turn at Eleusis,' Theo was saying. 'I had the story from an old peasant woman who had once been my mother's maid. Of course she had been sworn to secrecy, but somehow I always get these things out. They all go to the house of the midwife—but, of course, you know the story of Alcibiades and how he dressed up . . .' Theo's voice became louder and louder, and more and more animated as he strove, in vain, to recapture Götz's interest. 'We must go to Tirnavos together, Herr Joachim,' he concluded at last.

'What? Yes, yes . . . Let us do that.' Götz glanced round guiltily at us, and then resumed his contemplation of the two girls. Suddenly he said: 'I think I shall bathe.'

'Bathe! . . . But here is the fish,' Cecil protested.

'I shall only be a moment.'

'Have you got a towel?' Theo asked.

'No, I don't need a towel. I never use one.'

'And what about a costume?'

'I can wear my pants.'

Theo said genially: 'All right, all right. But be quick! Otherwise your fish will get cold.' He added, as Götz shambled off towards the bathing-cabins: 'The water certainly looks inviting.'

'You mean, those girls look inviting,' Cecil said sourly. 'Our friend seems to be an absolute satyr.' Like many people whose own sexual foibles call for toleration, Cecil was never tolerant towards the sexual foibles of others. Even to those who shared his own specialised tastes he was always saying contemptuously: 'But you're so indiscriminate—your range is as wide as an Aga cooker's'; or 'Of course, you're an absolute baby-snatcher', or 'But how could you—with a monster like that?' He added now: 'He doesn't seem to have a thought in his head except women.'

48

Götz had reappeared, his vast paws tucked under his naked arm-pits, as he picked his way, with bandaged feet, over the pebbles, tin-cans and shells that littered the sand. Naked except for a pair of pants which might either be a faded khaki or a grubby white, he looked even taller and skinnier and more albino than in his clothes. Even the hair that sprouted from his nipples and in a line down his breast-bone was of a pinkish tinge; his skin was the colour of lard. 'Ugh!' he said, shuddering. 'It's cold.'

'In you go,' Cecil said; and as Götz scampered off, he added: 'He suffers terribly from what Lord Palmerston used to call "esprit de corps".'

The girls were already bobbing up and down in the water, like a couple of celluloid dolls, emitting attenuated shrieks whenever the water rose above their waists. Götz began to swim round and round them, with powerful ungainly strokes which sent the spray glittering high into the air. He shouted something, either at them or at us, went far out and then swam back. Raising one paw, he all at once sent a vast billow cascading over their heads. They both screamed, and then gulped and coughed and spat and rubbed their smarting eyes as Götz went off into peal on peal of laughter. However, once they had recovered, they took no more notice but, with an ineffectual, wriggling breast-stroke, began to move away. Götz pursued, striding through the water, his long, lard-coloured arms held high above his head. Again he splashed, but this time he guffawed even before the water had swept over the girls; he continued to guffaw as once more they choked and put their hands to their eyes. Then one of them turned, and when she spoke, it was not

49

in Greek, as both he and we had expected, but in English with a peculiarly piercing Brooklyn accent:

'Would you get to hell out of here, mister? Or do you want me to kick your front teeth in?'

Götz floundered away towards us: his face was red and even his neck and bare shoulders were going a mottled pink. With long strides he began to emerge from the water, when suddenly the two girls went off into a shrill whinnying of laughter. Götz's pants had all at once slipped down to his ankles.

'That was a typical transatlantic reaction,' Theo said as Götz went into the bathing-hut to put on his clothes, 'that ill-bred and vulgar laughter. What, after all, is there comic about the human form? Do we laugh at the Venus di Milo? Once a country loses its sense of the dignity and beauty of the naked human animal, then it is indeed entering on a period of decadence. I imagine that those two sluts would have gone off into the same hysterical giggling when Ulysses appeared naked from the waves before Nausicaa or when Venus rose, as Botticelli painted her, from the foam about Cythera.'

After this incident Götz was as sulky towards us as if we ourselves had been responsible for his discomfiture. He sat, while we ate, staring moodily either at the table or in the direction of the two girls who were now once more outstretched on their deck-chairs, and though Theo would pass on to his plate all the best pieces of fish from his own—a real sacrifice, for Theo loved food and of all food, fish most of all—yet the German would do no more than take an occasional nibble. The salt had dried on his eyebrows and ears to make a kind of scab-like crust and the close-cropped hair of his head had so stuck together that it bristled from his scalp like the thorns on a gooseberry. Theo tried to woo him from his sullenness, not only with food, but with conversation: to no avail.

After we had finished the meal, Cecil got up. 'Well, I think I shall go for a stroll,' he announced. I knew from experience that if he wished to be accompanied, he would have said so.

'And I think I shall join you.' But as Theo struggled to his feet, Cecil pushed him back:

'No, I'd prefer to be alone.'

He wandered off; and I saw that he was making for a solitary fisherman so distant as to be almost invisible. There was no doubt that he had sharp eyes. Götz had undone one of the bandages on his feet and was pricking irritably at a blister, as Theo said: 'Well, I must be off on one of my little expeditions in search of raw material.' I wondered if his 'raw material' would be the same as Cecil's, but he added: 'I have so many orders for jewellery, and it's hard to find the right kind of shells. . . . Who's going to help me?'

Silence.

'Lazy boys!'

He shambled off into the bright spring sunshine; then, suddenly, he sat down on the sand and took off his shoes and socks, which he left behind him on a mound, and walked on, bare-footed. He had also taken off his small green beret and from time to time he would stoop, pick up a shell and, if he did not reject it after a close-sighted examination, would place it in this improvised receptacle. Götz and I watched him; I was almost half asleep. 'What is he doing?' Götz said at last. I told him. 'Ah!' Then he rose. 'I shall help.'

His khaki shirt fluttering loose about him, Götz strode out over the smooth sand. 'Hi!' he shouted. 'Hi!' The two men faced each other, Theo's hand raised to his forehead against the glare of the sun as he looked up at the German. Then they both set to work. Götz would patiently bring each shell he discovered to Theo for appraisal, and sometimes many minutes would pass as they discussed the colour of one or the shape of another. Sometimes Theo would raise a shell to Götz's ear or throat, or would put it to his finger, testing it in these contexts. They looked happy there together; happier certainly than Cecil who was wandering round his fisherman in ever-narrowing circles, like a distracted goat on a tether.

CHAPTER

3

WHEN I said goodbye to Theo and Cecil the next day, Theo urged me, as he shook my hand warmly: 'When you're next in Athens, you will of course come to stay with me, won't you? I can't offer you luxury, you know —I am a poor man, as Cecil has probably told you—but I can offer you quiet and freedom. Freedom, above all. . . . So please do come.'

I thanked him, touched by the warmth and spontaneity of this invitation to someone whom he had only known two days, but never guessing that within the next week I should find myself in a position to accept his hospitality. I was to have an operation: but I must confess that I thought neither of Theo nor of staying in his house as I made my preparations. At times of apprehension and physical distress I find luxury the most satisfactory of all anodynes and I planned either to stay at the Grande Bretagne while I was waiting to go into hospital or, if he could have me, at the home of my friend Dino Haralambos. Fortunately Dino's spare room was unoccupied and after the rudely uncomfortable life of my flat in Salonica, it was some consolation for the ordeal ahead to enjoy the pleasures of being valeted, taking baths at all hours of the day and drinking Dino's gin and whisky.

One evening, after some disagreeable hours in the X-ray department of the Evangelismus Hospital, Dino took me to Zonar's for a drink, and as we sat perched on two stools before the bar, Theo appeared. He did an evening round, as I later discovered, of all the bars and pastry-shops in Athens; but he never bought anything, and if he saw friends, he would usually refuse, out of pride, to accept anything from them. Instead, late at night, he would go to a milk shop where he would eat a plate of yoghourt before he retired.

He now peered short-sightedly round Zonar's door for several seconds before he saw I was there; then he hurried over, sweeping off his wide-brimmed grey felt hat, pinned up at one side like an Australian soldier's: 'Frank! What are you doing here? When did you arrive? How nice to see you, dear boy! . . . Good evening, Mr Haralambos.' He turned coldly to Dino, and Dino returned an equally cold: 'Good evening, Colonel Grecos.' I discovered later that the two men disliked each other. Theo used to say about Dino, who had finished his education at Balliol: 'Greeks must have the courage to be Greeks and not inferior imitations of Americans or Englishmen'; and Dino about Theo: 'Yes, I know Frank. I'm sure that he's the kindest man in the world. But Athens is not London—everyone knows everything about everyone else—and in my job I just can't afford to have my name linked with his.' (Dino worked in the Greek Foreign Service.)

Now I felt guilty and wondered how I should excuse myself to Theo for not having been to stay with him: I had already heard stories about his touchiness, and he would be hurt and contemptuous when he learned that I had preferred what he would consider to be the false Anglo-American comfort of Dino's household to the authentic Greek discomfort of his own. But it was he who was apologising: 'I expect it was you who telephoned this afternoon, wasn't it? Cecil said the 'phone rang, but he was—er—busy at that moment and could not go to answer it. The terrible thing is that unless you'd like to sleep on the sofa, I don't know where to put you. You see, I have Cecil in one spare room and in the other I have our German friend: he had nowhere to go in Athens and no money on him. What could I do? Of course, *if* I'd known that you'd be here . . .'

At this moment a filthy and palsied old man who had been moving among the tables peddling cigarettes and postcards tweaked Theo's sleeve. 'Excuse me a moment,' Theo said. He and the old man began to whisper in a corner, Theo lowering his head as the old man stood on tiptoe to put his toothless mouth up to his auditor's ear. 'You see what I mean,' Dino said. 'He's thoroughly disreputable.' He stared at his own handsome well-bred face in the tarnished mirror opposite him: in his stiff collar, blue-and-white striped shirt and Savile Row suit, he might have been any promising English diplomat. 'I wish I could afford to be disreputable now and then,' he sighed.

Theo showed an inexhaustible interest in all the details of my illness for he was, I discovered, one of those people whose hypochondria is directed, not inwards to themselves but outwards to their friends and their families. If

I had to make a laboratory test or see a specialist, he would insist on coming with me; and when I recovered consciousness, his was the first face I recognised. I opened my eyes and through the dreamily dispersing mist was aware of a number of silent white-clad forms motionless at the foot of my bed. I remember thinking, without any alarm, but in a contentment induced by the anaesthetic: 'There are at least a dozen doctors there. I must be really seriously ill.' Then I realised, with a shock, that these doctors were wearing pyjamas. They were not doctors, but patients from other wards, who had drifted in, unbidden, to watch me 'coming round'.

'How are you, my dear?'

'Theo. . . . Do tell these people to go away. What are they doing here?' I tried to sit up.

'Now don't excite yourself. You've been through a major operation—' Theo always insisted on thus dignifying my trivial ailment—'and now need all your strength.' He chuckled. 'I'll tell you later what you said when you were coming round. You were not at all the Puritan Maid that I had always taken you to be.' In actual fact, as I later discovered from my nurses, I had said nothing at all.

There always seem to be more doctors than nurses in Greek hospitals and late that evening when my surgeon came to visit me accompanied by some half-dozen assistants, Theo was among them. He stood as they stood, his hands clasped before him and his head slightly bowed, as the surgeon examined me; then, like them, he gave a nod of the head, while the surgeon said a few words, and afterwards treated me to a brief, yet sympathetic smile. The rôle had been perfectly sustained, even to the aside with which he told my nurse to straighten my pillow.

From then on, I saw much both of him and of Götz, though they rarely came together. Theo was fascinated by the life of this vast hospital and he would wander about the public wards on the same floor as mine, chat to the patients, nurses and doctors, and then come to me to tell me about some peculiarly atrocious discovery he had made. Götz, on the other hand, loathed the place; he had a morbid horror of disease and he told me that even the smell of the entrance made him feel faint and sick. It was, therefore, a real kindness that he visited me almost daily; while for Theo I suspect that such visits were as much a treat as a duty.

Each time that Götz called he would bring some small present. Once it was some oranges, wrapped in a screw of newspaper, which cascaded over the floor under the feet of my surgeon and his assistants who were examining me at that moment; on another occasion it was a bottle of Bovril which he had bought from one of the black market stalls and which turned out to be bad; on yet another occasion it was a completely unusable foot-rest which he himself had made when I complained that my heels were getting sore. We talked about English literature (about which he knew something) and about philosophy (about which I knew nothing) and about my night nurse. It was this last topic that really interested Götz.

Stavroula came from Boeotia and she amply justified the reputation for stupidity that the Boeotians enjoyed in classical times. It was she who dosed me with salts after I had been on sulphonamide drugs for three days; with disastrous results that mystified my doctors since I was reluctantly persuaded by her not to give her away. It was, needless to say, her hand that was holding the syringe on the only occasion when a needle has broken off in my flesh. And she, of course, was the nurse who had the reputation of giving enemas and forgetting to bring the bed-pan. She was a deeply religious girl, and if I ever complained of pain, would exhort me to pray. Her arms, when she rolled up her sleeves as she frequently did, were large and muscular, and covered with black hair; she was handsome, I suppose, in an ardent, provocative way, and Götz always maintained that the moustache on her upper lip only added to her attraction. To doctors and patients alike she exhibited all that jolly archness which seems to me the best argument for being nursed by nuns.

One day rumours had come to me through other patients, who were forever drifting into my room unasked, that Stavroula had been caught by Matron the previous night in the bath with one of the surgeons, a goat-like White Russian of over sixty. I did not need to be told that she was not in the bath for the sake of cleanliness; it was obvious that she had an aversion to water. In England I imagine that after such an incident both nurse and surgeon would never have been seen again; but apart from Stavroula's red eyes and perpetual sniff as she went about her tasks, and the overt mockery of the patients, there were no more serious consequences that I could note.

'Poor girl,' Götz exclaimed, when I told him the story. 'How horrible these Greeks are! He probably forced her to do it. And now I suppose they all despise her and look down their noses at her. What a country!'

At this moment Stavroula herself came in with the thermometer. She always refused to take my temperature in my mouth, and insisted on tucking it under my arm, on this occasion making a crude joke about the differences between the Greek, English and French methods. 'Time for beddy-byes,' she said (I translate the Greek into what seems to me the nearest English equivalent). She began to sweep all my papers off my bed, inextricably confusing them as Götz leapt up to help her; soon they had the appearance of fighting for the papers over my body. 'But keep them in order,' I protested. 'Keep them in order.' The papers, the beginnings of a new novel, were placed on the seat of the commode. Götz gave Stavroula a slow grin, and she looked back at him, her arms crossed over her ample bosom, with a challenging expression that seemed to demand: 'So what?' He pulled out a slab of chocolate from his pocket, and offered her some.

She tossed her head, and as she plucked the thermometer from under my arm, said: 'I don't want to spoil my supper.'

Götz looked humbled.

'Your friend will have to go now. I can't have him tiring you out.' What really tired me out, as Stavroula well knew, was her habit of playing the radio full on in the nurse's room beside mine. 'Tell him to run along now . . . I must give you your injection.' I winced at the thought of that indifferently jabbing needle, the discomfort of which was always accompanied by Stavroula singing to herself in her deep contralto. 'Tell him to run along, dear—come on!'

'He knows Greek.'

Götz was staring at Stavroula utterly bemused, but now he shook himself and picked up a pile of books he was returning to Dino for me. 'Sorry, Sister,' he said; it was obvious that, even in Greece, Stavroula would never be anything but a nurse. 'We're all glad that Mr Cauldwell finds himself in such competent hands. Well—we must soon get him well. And then the three of us ought to celebrate by going out together.' He was backing out of the door when there was a jangle and clatter as he collided with the trolley Stravroula had left outside.

'Mind my bottles,' she shrilled; and as Götz loped off, muttering apologies, she added: 'Idiot!'

'Your friend's not exactly a picture, is he?' she said, as she arrived with the syringe. 'Now over you go! . . . Oh, your poor little sit-upon!' She was dabbing with cotton-wool. 'I don't mind going out with you, Mr Cauldwell, of course—seeing that you've been my patient —but I must say I was surprised at that suggestion, coming from Mr Frankenstein.' I wanted to tell her that it was not Frankenstein, but his monster, who was hideous, but my face was in the pillow. 'Now then, keep still.' She began to trill a snatch from the film 'The Great Waltz' that had just been revived in Athens and then broke off to say: 'These needles they give me! I could use them for knitting. . . . Now, dear, perfectly still—perfectly still!' She jabbed, and then as she slowly withdrew the needle she said: 'Yes, I think he's cheeky—he's altogether a little too cheeky. *And* he could do with some plastic

surgery. . . . There we are!' The needle was at last out.
'Now, have you been a good boy today?'

I nodded; this was a euphemism that I particularly
detested.

'Really and truly?'

'Yes.'

'All right. . . . Now remember to say your prayers!
What would your mother in London think if she knew
that night after night you . . .'

I turned my face to the wall, and drew the blanket up
over my ears in an effort not to hear her. It seemed to me
one of life's typical ironies that whereas I, and most of the
other male patients on the floor, had perpetually to repel
Stavroula's advances, poor Götz's advances should in
turn be repelled by her.

By now I had reached a stage when, unless I thought
about it, I had ceased to notice Götz's ugliness; and on
occasions such as this, when Stavroula's distaste had
forced it on my notice, it only seemed to throw into
greater contrast the quite extraordinary simplicity and
goodness of his heart. Dino was equally generous, but
he was after all a rich man; Theo was equally attentive,
but, unlike Götz, so far from feeling horror, he enjoyed
visiting hospitals. Neither of the two men gave the
impression, as Götz did, of sympathy in its fullest Greek
sense; of suffering shared, so that one's own physical
aches and disabilities seemed to become another's.

But I shall be chiefly grateful to Götz for what may
appear to be two of the most trivial of kindnesses; for
giving me the only bed-bath I ever had in hospital and

for helping me to escape from hospital a week before I should. The bed-bath he gave me on the day on which I had my stitches removed. We had been playing chess, when the surgeon arrived, with his customary entourage of white-robed assistants, and Götz shambled, blushing, to his feet; unlike Theo, he was unable to face such a situation with anything but embarrassment and panic. 'Shall I go?' he asked, stumbling for the door.

'Your friend can wait on the balcony—in this wonderful spring sunshine,' my surgeon said in English. Then, as Götz went out, he turned to one of his assistants and murmured in Greek: 'Better shut the doors. If he yells, we don't want his friend to hear.'

I clenched my fists under the bedclothes and shut my eyes; I wished that, if I were going to yell, I might be allowed to do so before less of an audience. I began to count; conscious, at the same time, both of the cold sweat that was pricking through my skin, and of a fussing with my bandage. How long they were taking!

'There!' the surgeon said. Well, at least, the bandage was off; now would come the pain as the stitches were ripped out. I shut my eyes tighter, and clenched my teeth.

'All right!' the surgeon said. I heard instruments rattling ominously in a basin.

'All right!' he repeated. 'All over!' The stitches were already out.

There are many advantages in being ill, not in Greece, but in England; the doctors are better, the nurses more efficient, the hospitals cleaner. But there is one, to me insuperable, disadvantage: one is expected to be brave.

Götz was now by my bed, his face clammily green as he asked: 'Was it really awful?' He took my hand in one of his paws.

'Mr Cauldwell is the perfect patient,' the surgeon said. 'He has great physical courage.'

It was the first time that anyone had ever said that about me, and it will probably be the last.

Götz squeezed my hand again as the entourage filed out in order of seniority: 'Was it awful?' he asked again.

'Frankly, I didn't even know it was happening.'

'You're vonderful! You're so brave!'

'But I felt horribly ashamed of being so dirty. They all looked so clean.'

'Don't the nurses wash you?'

'No, never. I don't know whether it's laziness or excessive modesty. I suspect the former, posing as the latter.'

'Shall I wash you?'

'Oh, Götz, no—it'll be far too much trouble. Thank you all the same.' I had visions of being lifted up and down even more clumsily than when Stavroula made my bed; of water being splashed on to the blankets; even of being rolled on to the floor or having a basin spilled over me. Yet how wrong these imaginings were! Götz had worked in a military hospital in Germany during the war ('it was the most horrible, and yet the most vonderful experience of my life') and he now set to work with a skill and gentleness that none of my Greek nurses, and certainly not Stavroula, could ever hope to equal. He had taken off his tartan wind-jacket and there was a terrible pathos about the sweat-shirt which he wore underneath. Never had a garment been more aptly

63

named: it had once been navy blue but now, under the arms and round the neck, sweat had stained it the colour of rust. A hole in front had been clumsily drawn together into a tight knot with some ordinary black cotton, while behind another hole had been patched with what looked like a scrap from an old woollen vest. I felt an intense pity towards him, and hated myself for feeling it.

'How kind you are, Götz!'

He said nothing but, quietly absorbed, went on with his task of soaping my body.

I had hoped to leave hospital before the last week of Lent, but further complications had started and it now seemed as if I might even be there for Easter. Boredom and irritation set in. Instead of laughing at the cheerful inefficiency of the nurses, I now wanted to curse; my injections, instead of being an uncomfortable nuisance, had become a dreaded ordeal which prevented me from going to sleep; and, worse even than the sound of Stavroula playing the radio, church services had begun to be held in the corridors at all hours of the day and night. At first the nurses had wanted to wheel my bed out into the corridor so that I could be present at these services; then, when I refused, they would deliberately leave my door open so that all the sounds could reach me. Finally, when I used to shout for the door to be closed, they would ask the priest to call in on me before he left the floor; and I would blink up crossly at him, a book on my stomach, as he murmured some prayers, made the sign of the cross over me, and shook incense about the room, as though he were exorcising a devil. I became increasingly depressed.

'I shall never get out of here,' I said to Götz. 'And to-morrow is Good Friday. I was given boiled fish and yoghourt today, and yesterday, and the day before. Why should I have to fast? It's not even our Easter yet.'

Theo, who was with Götz, said: 'You sound just like a minor character in a Russian play.'

'We must get you out at once,' Götz said decisively. 'All you need is to be taken away from this place. Of course you can't get well here. . . . Where is your surgeon?'

'My surgeon?' It was then five o'clock in the evening.

'Is he still in hospital? And if not, where can we find him?'

'I suppose he's at home now.'

'Where is his home?'

I had never known Götz show so much decision.

'Voucharestiou 112. But, Götz, he'll never let me out.'

'Why not? I'll say that you want to be home for Easter. Every Greek understands that.' He lowered his enormous bulk on to my creaking bed and said earnestly: 'Look, Dino has said that as soon as you leave hospital, you can go straight to him. You'll be much more comfortable there, won't you?'

'Ye-es.'

'First point. Second point, I shall come and nurse you. I can do that better than Stavroula—can't I? Even if—' his face collapsed into a grin— 'there are some respects in which I cannot hope to equal her. Right?'

'Right,' I said dubiously.

'Good. Now you've finished your injections and you're out of danger. So there's really no reason why you shouldn't lie in bed at Dino's instead of here. Right?'

65

'Personally I think it's unwise to——' Theo began.

But Götz overwhelmed him. 'I shall go and see old Doctor what's-his-name now. You'd better come with me, Theo.'

More than an hour later Götz rushed into my room, followed by Theo; shouting: 'All right, you can go!' he began to fling my clothes into the suitcase he had dragged from under my bed. 'We've telephoned Dino, and everything will be ready. He's sending the car round.'

'Have you told the matron?'

'I told someone in the hall.'

'I think this is most unwise,' Theo said. 'Dr Kollia-copoulos was obviously doubtful whether, after a major operation like yours——'

'What a wonderful tie!' With an almost child-like pleasure Götz ran to the window and held it against his tartan wind-jacket, turning it this way and that so that the late evening sunlight glinted on the silk threads. 'It's beautiful.'

'Do you like it?' It had just arrived, belatedly, as a Christmas present from Italy. 'Somehow it doesn't suit me. You can have it, if you wish.'

'May I——? Oh, no, I couldn't! Really, I couldn't!'

'Don't be silly. Take it, please.'

After a brief tussle, Götz slipped the tie into his pocket and went on with the job of packing my things. A trolley jangled in the corridor outside, the door was flung open and Stavroula came in. She looked in amazement: 'What are you doing?' she demanded at last.

'Your patient is leaving you, Sister,' Götz said. He always blushed to a fiery red when confronted by her.

66

'What! . . . Are you mad? He's not leaving until next Monday.'

'Ring up and ask the doctor.'

'But he can't leave now.'

'Why not?'

'The male nurses are all off duty. How's he going to get to the lift? He can't walk there.'

'I shall carry him.'

As inevitably happens when there is an argument in Greece, other people now began to appear as though some sixth sense had drawn them to the scene. Patients, nurses, maids, visitors, even the barber with a silver jug of hot water steaming in one hand: one by one they looked in, listened and then added their voices to the general uproar. Götz continued to pack stolidly as they argued with each other. Finally, even a priest appeared, to rattle a collecting box before me.

When he had finished the packing, Götz handed the case to Theo and then, wrapping me in a blanket, lifted me in his arms and made for the door. Bound as in a cocoon, I felt like some monstrously over-grown baby. Stavroula rushed at me. 'Get down!' she shouted. 'Get back to bed! Do you want to kill yourself?' She began to pluck at the blanket about me in a feverish effort to catch hold of my arms. 'Let go!' Theo shouted at her, and she shouted back: 'You want to murder him! That's what it is—you want to murder him!'

Fortunately at this moment one of the women patients, who had been having a feud with Stavroula ever since she had accused the nurse of eating one of her chocolate biscuits, caught Stavroula from behind and tugged her away. I was swept out into the corridor, surrounded by a cheering, laughing, milling throng who accompanied me as far as the lift with cries, in both Greek and English, of: 'Good luck! Good health! Goodbye! Cheerio! Happy Easter!'

'I think I should have died there if you hadn't come to take me away, Götz,' I said.

Theo made a clicking noise with his tongue, his head on one side. 'I still think it was foolhardy,' he said. ' . . After a major operation like yours.'

4

THEO and Götz had been to a gramophone recital at the British Institute when I met them in the Zappeion Gardens; it was my second day out.

'Like all Germans, Götz is so fond of music,' Theo said. 'And, of course, as you probably know, composing is one of my artistic activities—one of my *many* artistic activities.' He linked one arm in Götz's and one in mine, as he smiled and said: 'Daphne Bath—*Lady* Bath, that is—called me the Leonardo of the Lycavettos. My street, you know, is Odos Lycavettos.'

'What did they play this evening?'

'Oh, British music, of course. Parts of that superb opera by that young man—what's he called?—Benjamin England, and then some Purcell, and then a modern concerto, to end with, about which Götz was quite crazy.'

'A modern concerto?'

'Yes, something to do with Prague or Sofia or one of those capitals behind the Iron Curtain.'

'Warsaw?'

'Yes, that's right: the Warsaw Concerto. Götz loved it. Didn't you, Götz?' He spoke to the German as though he were a small boy who had to be coaxed to display his brightness.

'Vonderful! Fantastic!'

'So you've found your way to our Zappeion, have you?' Theo said in a tone of playful insinuation. 'Ah, but it's not what it used to be! We've *la sottise* Peyrefitte and "Les Ambassades" to thank for that. The moment that book appeared, they began to talk about putting these wretched lights here. And the absurd thing is that we have power cuts in Athens! . . . Excuse me a moment.' He slipped off into the darkness under the trees in pursuit of some shadowy figure which might either be male or female.

'How are you enjoying life in Athens?' I asked Götz, whose face gleamed greyish green above me in a transverse beam of moonlight.

Götz sighed. 'There is so much,' he said, 'so much that is vonderful . . . But the one thing . . .' Again he sighed. Reaching up with his long arms he grasped the branch of a tree and swung himself back and forth. 'Have you a woman, Frank?'

Fortunately I was saved from having to answer this question by the return of Theo. He whispered something in Götz's ear and Götz at once brightened; again they whispered and I saw Theo pass Götz a note—it seemed to be for ten or twenty drachmae—which Götz first refused energetically and then at last accepted. 'All right—be off!' Theo gave him a push and Götz, his shadow leaping behind him, disappeared from sight.

Theo linked his arm in mine again: 'It's sad that these traces of Europeanism should cling to our friend. In so many ways he is *Greek*—I am sure that at heart he is

70

Greek—but on this particular subject he's so far from finding his true self.' He pressed my arm: 'And what is your true self? That is something we'd all like to discover.' I said nothing and he went on: 'Imagine that I'm your fairy god-mother. What would you like me to give you—here, now, in the Zappeion at this moment?'

'A nice strong cup of tea. I'm really quite exhausted.'

Theo looked momentarily put out; then he said: 'Come, let's take a taxi. But you'll have to pay for it. I gave my last scrap of money to Götz. I shall make you some tea at home. I think you will enjoy it. Usually I drink Earl Grey, but I am now trying a new blend: I believe it is called—' he thought for a moment—'Lyons. Yes, Lyons. I like that name. It sounds grand and regal and utterly British.'

I had always been told that Theo was a poor man, and therefore it was a surprise to find that his house was in that district of Athens which is called Kolonaki. Sandwiched between two immense, glittering blocks of flats (one of which, Theo told me, belonged to Dino's family) this ramshackle box with its sagging wooden balconies and Turkish style sash windows appeared either squalid or picturesque, according to the tastes of the observer. Theo obviously thought it picturesque as he let me into the shadowy courtyard, and I was inclined to agree with him. 'Dino's uncle keeps trying to buy my house from me. He doesn't like the house—one wouldn't expect him to like it—but he likes the site.' Theo chuckled. 'Well, he won't get it while I'm still alive. . . . Look at those monstrosities!' He waved his hand in the direction of one of the blocks of flats. '*Bauhaus!*'

Some rickety outside stairs led up to the front door which was on the first floor, and I had just begun to climb when I halted astonished. Standing in the doorway I could dimly see the enormous figure of a military policeman. He was wearing shorts, and his naked thighs and knees gleamed through the darkness. As I paused I heard Theo chuckle again beside me. 'Go on!' he said. ' He's not real!'

I then realised that this superhuman figure had been painted on the doorway.

'Tsarouchis did it for me. I particularly like the position of the knocker. That seems to me a good joke.' He gave a smart rat-tat, and then giggled. We both looked up at the square-jawed face, with the horizontal black line of its moustache, its eyes set close together and its high peasant cheek-bones; the same kind of stylisation had been achieved with the male Greek face as is achieved on the cover of *Esquire* with the American female one. On the bare forearms and thighs black hairs sprouted like the prickles on a cactus. In a corner was the single Greek word: Ela!

'You know what that means?' Theo asked. 'It's pleasantly ambiguous. It can be a challenge; it can be an invitation. "Come and get it" was Maurice Bowra's translation.' Theo sighed, and again banged the knocker. 'I feel he's an appropriate guardian to my shrine. . . . Enter, please!'

I accepted the invitation, but having once stepped into the hall, I looked about me in amazement. On one wall there was suspended an aeroplane propeller surmounted by two archaic Greek helmets and a straw boater which, Theo told me, had belonged to a young Etonian, the son of a former British Ambassador. On the other wall there was a long string of the masks which Greeks wear during the Carnival period, a picture by Zographos of the War of Independence, a photograph of Theo in a sailor suit at the age of eight, and a glass-covered case in which a number of regimental badges and buttons rested on red velvet. Everywhere there was dust and a strange sweet-sour odour.

'Go through to the sitting-room, my dear, and make yourself comfortable.'

But to make oneself comfortable in a room that is half a museum and half a junk-shop is not an easy task. Once again I looked in amazement about me, and once again Theo was delighted that I should do so. As I discovered later, he had some excellent pieces of furniture, many of them English, which he had saved from the old family home in Corfu; but every table and chair and desk was piled so high with the random accumulation of a life-time that one's immediate impression was one of unrelieved dirt and squalor. Then, slowly, objects detached themselves from the general murk and dust: a plate to celebrate the Coronation of King Edward VII; a French sailor's hat; an old-fashioned wooden camera, propped on an upright piano which was lacquered with roses; a beautiful Cretan ikon, which Dino had often tried to buy for his collection; a pottery horse as obscene as the position of the two riders seated upon it; a small copy of the Delphic Charioteer and innumerable surrealist objects made of plasticine, scraps of cloth and paper, sea-shells, vegetables, old hair-pins, picture postcards, buttons, stamps, and, indeed, any odds and ends that could ever have passed through Theo's hands. At these last I began to stare with an uncomprehending astonishment, going from one to another while Theo shuffled behind me.

At last he chuckled and said: 'This is my art.' He added as my bewilderment remained: 'This is my fantasiometry. . . . Here, for example, is the Baroness Schütz.' The face had been constructed with a brilliant economy out of a potato, now black with age, into which two jet hat-pins had been thrust to make eyes glittering malevolently on the end of their antennae. 'The hat-pins were, of course, her own. I purloined them when I went to tea at the German Embassy—entirely in the interest of my art, of course.' His blue eyes twinkled. 'The ribbon round the throat is also hers; I snipped it from one of her evening dresses—fortunately she did not notice. . . . Oh, and her hair is also hers—I got it from her hairdresser. Here she has only one breast, as you see—' he indicated a sea-shell— 'in fact, she had two. But I wanted to symbolise her Amazonian nature. . . . This, next to her—' he pointed to a dried frog from the head of which the main spring of a watch curled quivering upwards—'is Bakolas, the famous banker. You will see that I have had to mutilate this creature—' he turned the frog upside down—'as poor Bakolas, who was in love with the Baroness, suffered from a psychological impotence. . . . Ah, you're looking at the watch spring. That, of course, symbolises his fanatical precision—and it enters into his brain as, in the end, it drove the poor man mad. . . . Now who else

74

would interest you? That is one of those muddled, and not even always well-intentioned young Britishers who were dropped into this country by your Government in the war. The body, as you see, is made from a Gordon's gin bottle, and the face is a piece of what I believe you call "Lifebuoy" soap. There used to be a halo which was made of one of those gold sovereigns which you used to scatter with such generosity—thus permanently dislocating the whole economy of Greece—but alas, at an hour of need I had to go and sell it. . . . Yes, that's a German swastika on one cheek and a Communist hammer and sickle on the other—your policy there was always two-faced, if you will forgive my saying so. The blood-stained bit of rag lying at his feet I cut from a young man whom I found dead outside my house in the civil war. . . . The whole thing is, as proper, surmounted by a Union Jack.'

He continued to explain other objects at random, while I listened, amazed both by the patience and skill that had gone into their construction and by their dotty and often macabre appositeness. 'I regard myself as simultaneously a poet and a sculptor,' Theo declared at one moment; and there was a quality of inspiration about these extraordinary works that gave him the right to make that boast, in spite of their absurdity.

'But enough of this. You sit at the piano and play something, while I get the tea. . . . Cecil is in, but must not be disturbed,' he added in a whisper, pointing conspiratorially at a door that was half covered by a length of tattered and dirty William Morris curtain. He winked.

'But I don't play the piano.'

'Ah well—then amuse yourself in some other way. . . . Look through the keyhole, if you want to.'

I did not accept this invitation but instead took up the first magazine that came to my hand: it was called *Brüderschaft* and had been published in Hamburg in the August of the previous year. At least a quarter of it was devoted to advertisements, many of which had been circled with red pencil by some unknown hand.

Theo returned with a tray on which there were two chipped Crown Derby tea-cups, resting on white utility saucers, a battered tin tea-pot and what looked like a tea-cosy, made to resemble a thatched cottage out of coloured silks and raffia, standing not over the tea-pot but apparently on its own. He rummaged in a cupboard, scattering old magazines and letters to the floor, and at last produced a tin, with a Scottie painted on the lid, that contained petit-beurre biscuits moist and crumbling with age.

'Milk?'

'Yes, please.' Then I realised that there was no milk jug on the tray. 'Oh, don't bother. I'd just as soon have it without.'

Theo gave a smirk. 'No. You shall have milk. I was hoping you would ask for it.' Deliberately he poured the tea, and then, with the theatrical assurance of a conjurer revealing some surprise, he plucked the tea-cosy off the tray between thumb and forefinger.

Next to the tea-pot there now stood a large and realistic phallus which Theo raised, in a pretence of nonchalance, and inclined towards my tea-cup. The milk trickled out, and as it did so, he glanced up at me mis-

76

chievously from under his bushy eyebrows to see how I was taking the joke.

'But, Theo, where on earth did you get that object?'

'Peasant art, my dear. There was a man, in Peiraeus, who used to make them—alas, he's had a stroke, and his son, who has taken over from him, refuses to continue with that—er—line. It's charming, don't you think? And extremely practical. It unscrews here—rather like a cocktail shaker. Of course the Greeks wouldn't use it for milk, but for ouzo.' Ruminatively he ran the knobbly fingers of one hand over the gold fronds; then he said: 'I used to have three. I gave one to the wife of the former French Ambassador, and one I sold to an insufferable American who said he wanted it for the Anthropological Museum at Mexico City—I never really believed him. But this is the biggest, so of course I kept it for myself. . . . Do have another biscuit.'

'No, really, thank you.' One had been enough.

Theo sighed. 'That's a change I've noticed in the English. They used to eat tea; but now, when I have guests here, they never seem to want anything. . . . I wonder how Götz is doing? Poor boy!'

As he began to speak of the German with a kind of paternal sorrow—of his ugliness, and goodness, and of the women who repaid his devotion with jeers or demands for cash or merely indifference—I realised, for the first time, the extent of Theo's affection for the other man. He liked Cecil, he liked me, I could see; but this was something different—obsessive, all-embracing, unremitting in its ardour.

77

'He has made a great difference to my life,' Theo said. 'I don't like being alone—I never have. When my wife first left me, I almost went mad.' I was startled; I had never guessed that Theo had been married. 'Cecil has, of course, been here off and on these last two months, but that is another thing. He lives his own life and leaves me to live mine. He's generous to me, so I really shouldn't object if he regards my home as a maison de passe. But Götz—Götz is different, quite different. You see, he *relies* on me; that is the important point. And I—I have come to rely on him. I don't simply mean, of course, that he does so much about the house or even that he's been such a help to me with my work. It's more than just that. We really understand each other; we are, in a sense, complementary to each other.' He got up. 'Now let me play you the ninth movement of the Athens Concerto.' He opened the piano and, putting his left hand on his knee, began to rub it with his right. 'It was Götz who suggested this movement to me. Originally there were to be ten movements; now there will be eleven. This is to be called "The Tavern Dancers" and in the course of nineteen minutes you will hear—if you are clever—no less than sixty-nine different popular tunes. Quite a tour de force, eh?' He continued to rub his hands gleefully as he spun round on the piano stool to face me. 'You may not believe this, but I never had a music lesson in my whole life. I'm entirely self-taught. . . . Well, *andiamo*.' He spun back on the stool and scrabbled some arpeggios. Then, breaking off: 'You must understand, firstly, that the work is still in a fluid state, and, secondly, that I shall have to try to suggest to you the various instrumental

78

parts. My scoring is most elaborate,' he added with a certain self-satisfaction. 'Ready—steady—go!'

As in the case of his 'fantasiometry', so now, while he played, I felt that there was a certain dotty genius at work. By all conventional standards, the dissonance was horrible —Theo not only seemed incapable of hitting a note without smudging the notes on either side of it, but he also appeared to be under the impression that, in *fortissimo* passages, the loud pedal should be kept permanently down. From time to time he would shout out 'Flute!' 'Harp!' 'Bassoon!'; and would go 'Oompah! Oompah! Oompah!' for a few bars and then explain, in a dignified aside, 'That was the trombones'; would bang with a teaspoon on the tin tea-pot with his left hand as he hammered the tune with his right, hissing 'Cymbals, now—cymbals!'; would make a curious whistling sound from between half-closed teeth ('Wind-machine!'), or would merely hum, falsetto, swaying from side to side as he introduced yet another of his sixty-nine themes. It was an extraordinary performance.

'Drums!' he was shouting. 'Drums! More drums!' when, from the room next door, there came a noise as if heavy furniture were being dragged about and then flung to the floor. Theo glanced up, but went on playing. Another thump; yet another; the windows began to rattle.

'What's happening?' I shouted above the music. 'Is Cecil all right?'

Still playing, Theo nodded and gave me his boyishly mischievous grin. Then, modulating with surprising skill

79

into a bar from the Britten opera which he and Götz had heard at the British Institute, he chanted out: 'Grimes is at his exercise! Grimes is at his exercise!', following this up with peal upon peal of laughter.

Soon the bangs and thuds ceased; but Theo never succeeded in playing me the whole movement, since five minutes later Götz shambled in.

'Well, how did it go?' Theo broke off to ask.

Götz, his wind-jacket and hair stuck with dry twigs, shrugged his massive shoulders. 'As it always goes. Anticipation—pleasure—disgust.' He sank into a chair, which creaked noisily as he drew up his dusty plimsolls and curled himself into a ball. 'How I hate that argument about money,' he said moodily.

'But I'd fixed it all. I said ten drachmae to her.'

Götz sighed: 'Yes, but she thought I was an American —or English. So we had this awful shouting-match. . . . Oh, how sordid it all is. Aren't there any nice girls in Athens?'

'Of course there are,' Theo said soothingly. 'But you want everything in such a hurry.'

Götz picked irritably at a length of cord that had come loose from the upholstery of the chair. 'The truth is that nice girls aren't interested in me.'

'Now don't be silly. . . . Come—let me give you a cup of tea.' Theo patted him on the shoulder, and then looked up, startled; from the hall there came the sounds of two voices raised in angry altercation. 'Now what's happening?' he asked. One voice was shrill; the other rough and deep.

The front door slammed and Cecil, in slippers and

a silk kimono, embroidered with a dragon, swept in exclaiming: 'The cheek of it! The barefaced cheek of it!'

'Why, what's happened?'

'Oh, the usual! Of course I sent him packing—you can trust me for that.'

'I think you're a bit unreasonable,' Theo said mildly.

'Unreasonable? How unreasonable?' Cecil swung his plump legs over the arms of his chair. 'At my age one doesn't expect to have to play at being Father Christmas. Besides—there's the principle involved.'

'Then it's hardly fair to make friends with someone who expects you to be Father Christmas. Is it?'

'That's his look-out.'

'H'm.' Theo considered; then he went on in the same mild tone. 'After all, you're really taking advantage of the good nature of the Greeks. In London I bet you wouldn't dare to behave like that—you'd have your nose broken for you. Whereas no Greek would dream of knocking someone like you about. And so you get away with it.'

'Oh, shut up, Theo! Don't be such a prig.'

'After all, what *is* ten or twenty drachmae to you?'

'I tell you it's the principle, the principle!' Cecil muttered, rising angrily to his feet. 'Kindly remember that I'm only twenty-nine.' At that he flounced into his bedroom, where we could hear his dropping what sounded like shoes on the floor.

Theo went to the door and asked: 'Did you speak to him about the fashion parade?'

'No.'

'Oh, Cecil! I reminded you.'

81

Cecil reappeared, sulkily filing his nails. 'I could hardly start talking about a fashion parade when we were in the middle of that sort of argument—now could I?'

'But he was just the type I wanted. And he comes from Crete.'

'Well, it looks as if you'll have to find someone else—stinky boos to you,' Cecil said unhelpfully. He turned to me: 'Has Theo talked you into taking part?'

'Me? Taking part in what?'

'I haven't told you about it yet,' Theo said. 'Among my other accomplishments, I am a dress designer. A special sort of dress designer. And in ten days' time I shall have my first show. I was particularly hoping to get Cecil's—er—companion as one of my mannequins.' Eagerly he went on to explain to me that all his clothes were based on the Greek traditional costumes—'One of the greatest tragedies of the last fifty years has been the general adoption of European dress.' The fashion parade was to take place in Constitution Square at eleven o'clock one Sunday morning. He sighed: of course the initial cost had been enormous—he had had to scrape and pinch and, but for Cecil's generosity, he could never have even contemplated such an outlay—but he was sure that, having cast his bread upon the water, he would get it back a hundred-fold.

'Would you like to take part in the parade—as Cecil suggests?'

Hurriedly I excused myself: during this period of convalescence I had to take things easy and, anyway, I was always self-conscious on such occasions, I explained.

'Do you think Dino would help? I have one model—

what we call a "smoking" and you call a "dinner jacket"
—which he would carry off to perfection. You see, for
ordinary, everyday costumes I have a number of soldiers
and sailors and workmen who are going to look quite
splendid, but for evening dress one wants someone with
breeding and presence. I think Dino would be marvellous.
Let me show you the costume.' He went to a wardrobe:
'As you see, I have substituted the traditional fustanella for
the black trousers, and instead of the black tie there is this
hand-embroidered kerchief from the island of Scyros.
Don't you think that would look magnificent on a man
with Dino's legs?'

I doubted whether Dino would be willing to appear in
the most fashionable square in Athens in what looked like
a ballet dancer's 'tutu', however fine his legs, but I
promised to give him Theo's message.

'Of course I'm sending out invitations to everyone I
know. You must tell all your friends to come, won't you?
If you give me the names of any people you think might
be interested, I'll see that they receive invitations.'

I mentioned the Representative of the British Council
who would, I thought, appreciate the humour of the
parade, and a friend in the American Mission, but Theo
said airily: 'Oh, naturally, those sort of V.I.P.s are personal
friends of mine and will turn up anyway. . . . No, I was
thinking of some of the *dimmer* members of the Anglo-
American colony—Embassy clerks, and that sort of thing.
I'm awfully out of touch with that crowd. . . . When
you have a moment, do draw me up a list.'

It was Dino who explained to me, when I returned
home to dinner, that this fashion parade was by no means

the first attempt made by Theo to establish himself as something more than a 'character' in Athens. He knew that, if he were to die at that moment, he would be remembered as an amiable eccentric, about whom had accreted a large number of scandalous legends. But he was thirsty for a more durable fame than that. In middle age he had imagined that his early fame as an aviator would, at least, remain: but in an era of jet propulsion his exploits in his rickety Tiger Moth had already dimmed into oblivion. He would be a composer; or a poet; or an artist. Or, better still, he would be the last Universal Man, whose incredible scope would embrace all the sciences and arts as Leonardo had done before him.

Poor Theo! Inevitably, the parade was a dismal failure. Dino, as I had expected, refused to take part, and when I had passed this message on to Theo, was rewarded with a parcel that Theo himself handed to the man-servant while we were eating breakfast. 'Oh, this is too silly!' Dino exclaimed. Inside the cardboard box lay a bundle of thistles.

'What does it mean?'

'Donkeys eat thistles. Could that be it?'

We both began laughing.

'How did Dino like my little gift?' Theo asked, when we next met.

'What was the point?'

Theo giggled: 'Oh, surely you know enough about fantasiometry to guess what was the point! . . . Was he very angry?'

'No, I don't think so.'

'Oh.' Theo was plainly disappointed. 'Of course one

thing he learnt in England was how to hide his feelings.
I expect he was really furious.'

'He told me to tell you that you ought to change the
day you've chosen for your parade. You know, I suppose,
that on the same Sunday they're going to unveil the
Commonwealth Memorial?'

'Well—what's that to me? Who wants to go and see a
potty old Memorial unveiled? Anyway, I announced my
Parade first.'

'Most officials will *have* to go to the unveiling of the
Memorial. Monty will be there——'

'No Greeks will turn out to look at *him*.'

'And Lord Halifax.'

Theo mused. 'Now *he* would look superb in that
dinner jacket. Really quite superb.'

'Honestly, Theo, I think you should change the
day.'

'But how can I change it? I've printed my invitations.
I've sent most of them out. My friend, the Greek Ambassador in Ankara, has specially taken leave. I can't post-
pone the Parade at such short notice. Anyway it will be
only the military big-wigs who will go to the unveiling—
the smart and artistic people won't be interested in that
sort of nonsense. Will they?'

I continued to look doubtful.

'No, I am sure that it's we who will get the crowds.'

The fashion parade can best be described in Theo's one
word, as he put his hand on to the marble top of the
Grande Bretagne bar and burst into sobs: 'Fiasco!' he
groaned. Only half the costumes had been ready in time,
even though Götz had himself joined the two seamstresses

engaged by Theo, and of the dozen mannequins only five turned up: a waiter, who had to disappear before he could show his costume as he was wanted for duty at twelve o'clock; an elderly man, whose right leg was longer than his left, deputising for a cousin; two youths who giggled, emitted shrill screams and fought over everything they excitedly pulled on; and a Commando who stolidly refused to do anything until he was paid twenty drachmae, cash down. In the end, Götz and Theo had themselves to struggle into costume—Götz into some baggy Cretan trousers, and Theo into a modernised version of an evzone's dress—while Cecil and I feebly resisted their efforts to persuade us to join them. 'If you think you're going to get me prancing up and down the pavement outside the King George, making an ass of myself, you're bloody well mistaken!' Cecil succinctly summed up his own and my feelings.

'But what's happened to the other mannequins?' I asked.

'They've all had to go on duty at the unveiling. . . . I knew it would be a mistake to choose soldiers. I knew it all along! . . . Frank, do just run out and tell the police to clear a way for us. I've explained to them our route.'

I went out: but there was no need to have a way cleared. I had never seen Constitution Square so absolutely empty.

The parade started: a couple of shoe-shine boys ran after Götz making obscene comments about the Cretan trousers; the two giggling youths twirled and assumed extravagant poses before the few people drinking coffee or ouzo on the pavement outside the King George Hotel, reminding me, as they did so, of the girls I had once seen showing dresses in the restaurant of Marshall and Snel-grove; Theo cuffed a child on the head, when he tweaked his fustanella—the old man's face was bleak with a mingling of disappointment and aristocratic scorn; the substitute caught the longer of his two legs on an uneven-ness in the pavement and fell to the ground amid jeers and laughter; while, all the time, the Commando ran from me to Cecil, to Götz, to Theo, declaring that for ten drachmae—for ten drachmae only, cash down—he would wear anything we liked, anything at all.

'That wretched unveiling!' Theo now groaned. 'Oh, damn Montgomery! Damn Halifax! Damn them, damn them, damn them!'

As I learned from Dino at lunch, the unveiling had been quite as much of a fiasco as our Parade. British marines crashed, fainting, to the ground to the amusement of the populace; the joined British and Greek flags got stuck on the aegis of Athens, and after repeated tuggings by almost every important person present, a ladder had to be fetched before the Memorial could be disclosed; there was a gasp of relief and pleasure when, at long last, the figure stood glittering in the sunlight, followed at once by another gasp of horror from the English—at the base was the 1066-and-all-that inscription: 'Honey soit qui mal y pense . . .'

Naturally Dino's account of this greater fiasco could in no way console Theo for his own.

FOR the next ten days Theo seemed to be exhausted
and depressed. One no longer saw him making his round
of the bars in the evening, and when one went to visit
him, instead of holding forth with his usual garrulity and
vehemence, he would merely sit silent on a straight-
backed chair and revolve the ring, which he had once
declared represented the Marriage of Heaven and Hell,
about his knobbly finger. Götz would bring him cups of
tea, one after another, in endless succession, but even the
sight of the vast German pouring milk from the phallus
failed to induce a smile. From time to time he would
rattle his teaspoon in the cup, sigh heavily and murmur:
'Ah yes—yes—yes.'

'What's the matter, Theo?' Cecil asked during one of
these stricken afternoons.

'Oh, I feel old—so old.' Then he pulled himself
together and said: 'To be precise, this is one of my
depressive periods. Once the manic phase starts, I shall be
all right again. Then I shall show them! Yes, I still have
one or two surprises hidden up my sleeve. But now—I
must stay in the wilderness. Now I must prepare.'

It was the longest speech we had heard him make since
the fiasco of the Parade, and he concluded it with another

rattle of his teaspoon, another sigh, and another long-drawn 'Ah, yes—yes—yes.' Then viciously he muttered: 'But money is the worm that is curled round the heart of life. Money, money, money!'

'Now don't start worrying about money again,' Götz said soothingly.

'Why shouldn't I worry? Why shouldn't I?' With a magnificently tragic gesture Theo raised both his hands; then he let them fall back on to his knees, as he cried: 'How can I think of anything else, when those bills pour in and I don't even know how to look for my daily bread? And then that damnable woman keeps asking me to help her—' the 'damnable woman', I discovered later, was Theo's wife—'as if she hadn't already run through two fortunes of her own and one and a half of mine.'

'Sell the house,' Cecil said briefly. As he spoke there was a knock at the front door, three shorts and a long, and he jumped to his feet. 'That must be for me. It's the one I met at the News Cinema, I think.'

'Sell the house!' Theo muttered angrily as Cecil disappeared. 'That's just the sort of advice one would expect from him, the—the *sissy*!' He brought out the last word as if it were the vilest of abuse. 'If you knew, Frank, how ashamed I was when I had to sell our property in Corfu. As you probably know—though we no longer give ourselves titles in Greece—I really have the right to call myself the Conte di Greco. A Venetian creation, of course. Well, there was that superb house full of some of the most beautiful furniture in Europe—Venetian and English Regency and Louis Quinze—and who bought it? Who bought it? A Greek American who made a fortune out

89

of Motels—whatever they can be—in Texas! In Texas, Frank! . . . Ah—yes—yes—yes . . . And if it hadn't been for that damnable woman . . .' He shook his head from side to side, drawing down the corner of his mouth into a grimace of melancholy disgust.

'You shouldn't speak about her like that,' Götz said.

'Why shouldn't I speak about her like that? She's my wife, isn't she?' Then, no less suddenly, his exasperation flickered out, as he turned to pat Götz's hand: 'You're a good boy, Götz. You're a decent boy. And you're right —I shouldn't talk about her like that. I've done her many wrongs; and the worst wrong of all was when I married her.'

'But you've always said that she married you only because she wanted Greek citizenship,' Götz protested.

Theo was momentarily put out: 'Did I ever say that?' he demanded peevishly. 'Well, there you see! That's the way I talk about a woman to whom I've brought nothing but suffering and humiliation. I remember Gide once saying to me——' Theo was always quoting remarks made to him by eminent men; to this day I am not certain whether they were genuine or not—' "Théo," he said—we met in the Belgian Congo, incidentally— "Théo, all my life my wife has been my conscience." Those were his words—how clearly I recall them! And what was true of Gide's wife is so much more true of Nadia. Through all these long years, whether we have passed them together or apart, she has always been my conscience.'

I was anxious to meet Theo's 'conscience'; but the

opportunity did not come until some ten days later. I had more than once told Theo that when he next visited his wife, I should like to go with him, and he had assented: 'Yes, you must meet my dear Nadia. A remarkable woman—a remarkable woman, *in many ways*.' There was something slightly ominous in the emphasis he gave to these last three words.

One afternoon I came into the sitting-room to find him alone in a chair, his scarf knotted about his scrawny neck, his stained and moth-eaten overcoat on, and a tall, grey felt hat, stuck with a peacock's feather, pulled over his eyes. A large brown envelope rested across his knees, and his hands rested on the envelope. He was deep in thought. 'Ah!' he exclaimed, as I entered. 'Ah!' I was given no other greeting.

'Were you going out?' I enquired politely.

'I *was* going out. But I shall not go out now.' He shook himself and rose to his feet. 'Forgive my air of abstraction, dear Frank. I was making some calculations in my head, and since I have never been good at arithmetic, the effort has exhausted me. Sit down, sit down! I am delighted to hear that you have managed to get some work in Athens. You will have some sherry, won't you?'

I shook my head, knowing by now that Theo, like most Greeks, thought that sherry was the same as cherry brandy.

'I was going to call on my wife. I have something here that I think will give her pleasure.' He shook the envelope in the air.

'Money?' I remembered now that, as Theo's old woman

had let me in, I had noticed that the two archaic Greek helmets were no longer hanging in their usual place in the hall.

'Yes, money. One, or rather two, of my—er—ships have fortunately come home. So I am going to take Nadia half of the spoils. But I can't go. I've just realised that today is her birthday.'

This seemed to me a curious reason, and I said so.

'Ah, you don't understand. Nadia never celebrates her birthdays. One is not even allowed to mention them to her. And if I arrive with this money, today of all days, well, don't you see, it will look as if I intend it as a birthday present. And that will make her furious.'

I looked wholly mystified.

'You still don't understand,' Theo said. 'It's quite simple really. Nadia thinks that if we acknowledge that the years are passing, well, of course we grow old. But if we refuse to count them . . .' He broke off: 'Surely you see?'

'Is she a Christian Scientist?' I asked.

'Well—kind of,' Theo said doubtfully. 'Anyway you must get her to tell you herself. But not today—definitely not today. We'll have to go tomorrow.'

Nadia Grecou lived in a small, costly flat in a street that ran down off Kolonaki Square. A White Russian, she was one of those ageing women of whom people always say: 'Ah, she must have been a real beauty when she was young,' but who, in reality, have each year more and more to offer the world in elegance and grace and charm as each year the world expects less and less of them.

French had been her first language and she spoke both Greek and English inaccurately with a heavy French accent. She had a thin, slightly fox-like face with a pointed nose and chin, an over-wide mouth and grey eyes that were melancholy except when they flashed into a sudden, violent merriment or scorn. The extraordinary thing about her was her complexion, which was still that of a young girl in its delicate white and pink. Her hair, I guessed, had been artfully tinted to its chestnut colour, lying close to her small, bony head in a fashion that was reminiscent of the middle twenties. A number of rings flashed on her expressive hands which were being perpetually waved in the air.

She herself opened the door to us, revealing to the first glance the kind of hard, bright, anonymous interior to which one grows so accustomed in modern flats in Athens: but on a closer inspection I saw that everywhere there were signed photographs—of royalty, of actors and actresses, of famous jockeys and boxers and politicians— their silver frames glittering among the white furnishings and upholstery. Although it was still sunny outside, the curtains had been drawn; one felt that they had probably been drawn all day.

'So this is your young Englishman.' I was not sure that I really liked the 'your'. 'Theo tells me that you are a writer.'

'Yes—I do write,' I said lamely.

'Excellent. There's something I want you to look at for me, if you would be so kind. I'd rather you didn't take it away, as I have only one copy. I don't want advice on what's *in* it, you understand, but only on the English.'

She gave her exquisite smile: 'My spelling is terrible!
. . . Still, come and sit down—we can talk about that
later.'

The tea was already out on a table before the fireplace,
and Nadia Grecou now plugged an electric kettle into
the wall.

'Where's Maria?' Theo asked. 'Is it her day off?'

'She is away,' Nadia Grecou said shortly. Then she
added, with emphasis: 'But she will be back.'

'Oh,' Theo said. He caught my eye at the same moment,
and I had the impression that he gave me a lightning
wink. 'That reminds me. I brought this along for you.'
He drew the long brown envelope out of his breast
pocket and held it out to Nadia.

She stared down at it for a moment, and then her arm
shot out from under its draping of chiffon. She snatched.
Eagerly she tore the envelope and scrabbled through the
notes: her beautiful tranquil face was momentarily contorted with rapacity, as though a sudden squall had
flicked over a lake. She got up, unlocked a drawer of her
desk, and put the envelope in. When she returned her
face was once more smooth and expressionless. She had
never said a word of thanks.

'I wish I could have brought more,' Theo sighed.
'But I'm a poor man, Nadia—a very poor man.'

'Don't talk like that!' All at once she stiffened, looking
bony and rigid under the flowing draperies. 'How can
you expect to be anything but poor when you refuse to
hold the thought of being rich. Hold the thought, Theo
—hold the thought!' She herself, as I discovered later,
had so successfully held the thought of being rich that

even at their moments of greatest financial crisis she had refused to make any cuts in her standards of life.

Theo, looking humbled by her scolding, began to prepare the tea.

Nadia Grecou was not an unintelligent woman, as her conversation now revealed, and she had a certain grandeur which impressed itself on one and made one accept from her remarks which one would not accept without offence from another woman. She knew a great deal about English and French literature of the nineteenth century, German romantic music and the art of the Italian Renaissance. But she was scornful when one mentioned even a painter now so popularly accepted as Vincent van Gogh or a composer as Ravel. 'If that is the kind of thing you like, Mr Cauldwell, you must meet the little son of the caretaker of this block of flats. He was born without hands, and he is a hunchback, and he has no hair.' There was a certain gusto in the way she brought out these repulsive physical details. 'If you like the ugliness of Picasso, you will like his ugliness too.'

'Perhaps.'

'I am afraid I am old-fashioned, and prefer Beauty.' She saw that I had finished my cup of tea, and without offering me a second, she retired to the desk to fetch me her manuscript. 'It's only—' she flicked through the sheets—'forty-three pages. It's a play I have written in verse for the B.B.C. . . . Now come and sit here by the light.' Obediently I got up. 'But don't, please, mark the typescript. Just note anything you want on this piece of paper.'

'You will be in a draught there,' Theo said. 'You know you had lumbago yesterday.'

'Theo!' She gave what I can only call a snarl: at the moment I would not have been surprised to see her take a bite out of his leg. 'Don't talk like that! Why will you persist in willing illnesses on to others? I'm convinced that all your troubles are basically due to that kind of wrong thinking. . . . Pay no attention to him, Mr Cauldwell. Come and sit here.' I sat down in the draught; and whether because of the draught or Theo's wrong thinking, I had lumbago the next day.

'A Cretan Romeo and Juliet,' I read. 'A Tragedy in Poetry for Radio. Specially written for the B.B.C. Third Programme by Mrs Nadia Korchinska Grecou (Diploma in Fine Arts of the Athens Polytechnic).' I turned over and saw that the whole of the first page was occupied by the Narrator; and the second; and the third; and the fourth . . .

'Have you read as far as that?' Nadia's voice sternly asked from behind my shoulder.

'No, I was just trying to get some idea of the shape of the whole thing,' I stammered.

'Oh, I see. . . . You know the story, of course—you must have read it in the papers?'

'You mean, about the ——'

'The two families who have a feud, and the young man of one family who abducts the daughter of the other—you've read about that, haven't you?'

'Yes, I——'

'Oh well, it doesn't matter if you haven't. The play speaks for itself.' Laboriously I began to read through the first page: mis-spelled, written in a curiously stilted and foreign idiom, and twisted into couplets that reminded me of pantomime, the lines blurred before me into an incomprehensible mass. Nadia tapped with the nail of her right forefinger on the seventh line: 'You see the reference there?' she demanded.

'The reference?'

'You have read Hugo, haven't you?'

'A little.'

'Well, you know the line about "la mer sonore", don't you?'

'Oh, yes—yes,' I said feebly. I had never heard the line.

'Here we have cow-bells—' again the nail tapped— 'and here—very simple—a single sheep neighing. You do say neighing of a sheep?'

'Bleating.'

'A single sheep bleating. I imagine the B.B.C. can produce that kind of sound quite easily?'

'Quite easily.'

'Of course it mustn't be too realistic. It must be— *poetic*.' Her white hands fluttered delicately in the air; the chiffon billowed round her.

So it continued.

'You've spelled "apple" with only one "p".'

'Oh, what a pedant you are, Mr Cauldwell!'

'But I thought that was the kind of mistake you wanted me to point out to you.'

'Do you think the people on the Third Programme will like it?'

'There's no way of telling.'

Fortunately she all at once looked at her watch and

gave a small scream: 'A-i-i! I'm already ten minutes late for my bridge. Come, you must go! Let us all go together. But you will return another day, Mr Cauldwell.' She went into the next room and minutes passed as we waited for her to finish her preparations. Theo walked up and down the small room, from time to time smiling at me indulgently. Once he waved a hand in the air and said 'Exquisite taste'. Then he whispered: 'I must try to find that maid of hers and tell her to come back—now that there's some money with which to pay her.'

'Then it's not her day off?' I queried ingenuously.

'Sh! No wrong thinking!' And Theo began to giggle into his khaki handkerchief at his joke.

In the lift, Nadia asked Theo, for the first time that afternoon, how he was keeping. 'Oh, one mustn't complain,' he sighed.

'You're happy,' she said, not as a question, but as an affirmative statement which she obviously did not intend him to contradict.

'Who can say? I have my house and my possessions and my music and my fantasiometry. Above all—' he put a hand on my shoulder as the lift hissed to a stop—'I have my dear friends. But money—that's what always worries me.'

'But, Theo, why don't you sell the house?'

'Never.'

'In ten years' time it will have fallen to the ground anyway. It's not as if it were a particularly beautiful house,' she added. I imagined that for Nadia a 'particularly beautiful house' would probably turn out to be one of those overgrown Swiss chalets or shrunken Monte Carlo casinos so popular in the suburbs round Athens. 'If you sell it now, you would realise some money and could also insist on being given an apartment for as long as the block of flats stands.'

'No!'

'Oh, don't be so obstinate! What possible reason can you have for wishing to hang on in that old ruin?'

They continued to wrangle with increasing bitterness until we had to cross Stadium Street which, at this hour, is always thick with traffic. Nadia, with complete recklessness, stepped off the pavement and, with cars hooting, brakes screeching and bicycle bells ringing all about her, began to walk, slowly and in an absolutely straight line, to the other side. Her head, held wonderfully straight in its close-fitting grey hat trimmed with ostrich feathers, her feet in their elegant high-heeled shoes, and the general elasticity and vigour of her movements all suggested, at this distance, a woman of thirty. Theo was dithering: he caught my arm, as if to drag me to the same catastrophe with him, as a tram thundered towards us, and then pulled me back. Again he ventured forward. This happened three or four times until, suddenly, he lowered his head, as I had seen him do in Salonica, and scuttled over the road.

'And about time too!' Nadia greeted us. 'I've never seen such a cowardly exhibition.'

'Something should be done about this traffic,' Theo grumbled. 'It's all these wretched Americans with their cars like hotel suites on wheels.' Theo, like most Greeks, ascribed most of the difficulties of life either to past British, or present American follies. 'But, Nadia, you really must be a little more careful. You might have been run over.'

'Theo! I forbid you to do that! How dare you? Do you want to murder me?' Her small face was contorted and white under its make-up; she stamped one of her feet. 'How can I live when you keep pressing those horrible *errors* on me? If you are going to talk like that, it's better for us not to see each other. I will *not* be the victim of your fears and wrong thinking. I've told you that before.'

'I'm sorry, Nadia,' Theo said humbly.

'Apologies are not enough. You must change your whole attitude of mind. You have no idea what harm people like you inflict. . . . Goodbye, Mr Cauldwell. I shall leave a message with Theo when you must next call about the play.' I found myself saying thank-you. 'Goodbye, Theo—and remember—no wrong thinking!'

Theo watched her as she rapidly walked up the steps of a block of flats that looked like an enormous upturned concertina. Then he turned, and the expression on his face was an odd mingling of admiration, exasperation and hurt feelings. 'What a woman!' he said. 'How young she looks! What charm, what elegance, what savoir faire! . . . And what intelligence, too! I've no doubt that if she had really set her mind to it she could have been one of the world's greatest writers. Don't you agree?'

I made no reply.

AS I have so far recounted this story I have probably given the impression that my relations with Theo were always amiable and smooth: but I doubt if Theo's relations with anyone, except Götz, had ever been only that. In proportion as he cared for a person, so his fury was the more intense at some imagined slight or ingratitude; and it was not, unfortunately, difficult to appear to him to have been guilty of slights or ingratitudes. He was a man capable of any sacrifices for his friends; but in return he expected a similar willingness to make sacrifices. He lived, as he often said, for his 'little circle'; his 'little circle' must live, in turn, for him.

For Götz this was easy; he had a few acquaintances but no other friends and, except when he was in fruitless pursuit of some woman, his time was always Theo's. But for Cecil and myself it was always difficult to avoid being accused of treachery or time-serving. Each of us had other friends and interests, and I had my work. We enjoyed Theo's company but we also enjoyed the company of other friends of ours who were unlikely to appreciate him or be, in their turn, appreciated. Yet, whenever we spent a day without going out with him, the next day we would, at best, have to face his coldly silent disapproval or, at worst, make a superfluous defence of our friends and ourselves against the vehemence of his attack.

Most mornings he would telephone me, and I give the following as typical of such daily conversations:

'Shall I be seeing you today, my dear?'

'I'm not sure. I think I shall be awfully busy.'

'Waiting to see what will come along, eh?' Theo chuckled to take the nastiness out of the words. 'Where are you lunching?'

'Oh, at home.'

'I can understand your preference for Dino's French cook. . . . By the way, how is Dino?'

'He's writing letters at the desk beside me.'

'Give him my—er—regards. . . . Tell me, how did his party go?'

'His party?'

'I heard about it from Nondas Spiliotopoulos. . . . Wasn't that the day when you said you wanted a quiet evening at home?'

'It wasn't a party. We asked in one or two people.'

'So I shan't see you at lunch. And I suppose you're invited to one of your smart tea parties.'

'Not smart at all. I'm having tea with two old nannies.'

I could hear him making 'Tsk-Tsk!' at the other end of the telephone. 'You won't get far up the social ladder if you do that sort of thing. What about dinner?'

'Dino and I are going to the Galistras.'

'Better, much better. Up—and up—and up . . .'

Usually, now that I was giving lessons, it was in the evenings that we met; and such meetings would invariably resolve themselves into one of two patterns. Either we would sit in his house, drinking tea or cheap cognac and eating Turkish sweets which tasted like wads of tissue paper soaked in thick syrup; or we would go to a taverna, usually in Peiraeus. If we stayed at home, the evening rarely passed without Theo playing us some part of his Concerto, Götz whistling from the window at the girls who passed below, and Cecil sending me to tell some unwelcome soldier or sailor that he had come to the wrong address. Cecil was always making dates with what he would call 'monsters' whom he would then have to avoid.

If we went to a taverna, we usually took a taxi for which Cecil and I would pay. Theo would say 'I hear that the Arachova'—or 'Machi's', or the 'Katakosmo'—'is likely to be *interesting* this evening,' and we would usually go where he suggested: but since the things that were likely to interest Cecil would not interest Götz—and vice versa—I was never sure what Theo meant by this word. They were happy evenings; though when I think of the spongy liver we used to be brought to eat (it was probably spleen), of the resinated wine, a drink for which I have never acquired a taste, of the hiss and grind of the gramophone blaring out pre-war jazz or Greek popular songs, of the dust rising from the floor as the dancers shuffled round and the penetrating odours of charcoal, sweat and cigarette smoke, I find it hard to say why such evenings should have been so happy. As always in Greece, I suppose it was the people who made the difference. These artisans and sailors and soldiers would send us over a can of wine and, having drunk to their health, we would send them a can back. Cecil would invite some of them to join us or would watch, with a kind of moody intensity, as one or a couple would perform a traditional dance. 'Extraordinary, the grace of these lumbering peasants,' he would often say. It was a thing which never ceased to surprise him.

'They are possessed,' Theo would reply.

Certainly, as the dancers gyrated with bowed heads and ceaselessly clicking fingers, they gave the impression of a trance-like activity.

'But what a pity they don't keep their heads up, like Spanish dancers,' Cecil remarked.

'One must be humble before the mystery of artistic possession,' Theo said sententiously.

'Oh, come!'

Theo thought again; then he added: 'The earth is our mother and we look to her as we dance.' At this moment one of the dancers struck the earth with the palm of his hand: 'And we strike her in order to take strength from her.' Cecil scoffed at what he obviously regarded as an explanation of the moment, but Theo continued with a kind of hurt patience: 'You have read, of course, of how Hercules had to lift the giant Antaeus from the ground before he could overcome him? That was because the giant derived his strength from his mother, the earth.' Whenever one began to suspect that Theo's folklore had no genuine basis of scholarship, he would somehow be able to confute one's doubts in this way.

'Dance, Theo, dance!' Götz would now cry.

The old man would shake his head and smile down at the glass of retsina into which he was dropping pieces of apple to soak. 'Let me get drunk first. Unfortunately I have many inhibitions.'

Theo danced beautifully; and those who would at first smile or even openly mock at the spectacle of the old man marching stiffly on to the floor, removing his hat and coat which he would hand to the waiter, and then calling for the music he wanted, would shout out 'With your good health!' and send him over a carafe of wine as soon as he had ended. When he danced, he moved with an extraordinary dignity and calm and grace, wholly unlike the rigid, jerky manner in which he normally walked.

Götz also sometimes danced; but it was invariably a performance the clumsiness and absurdity of which—his legs were perpetually getting tangled in each other—had too much in it of pathos to be amusing to witness. His pink-blond hair would fall into his blinking eyes, his shirt would come out behind, and his harelip would be puffed in and out as he painfully gasped for breath. Nobody laughed at him; nobody had the heart to do so. All the customers in the taverna would keep their eyes averted from the dance-floor until he had finished.

Usually such evenings ended with our retiring to Theo's house in a taxi that carried, not only us, but at least one stranger: a taciturn evzone, perhaps, who only smiled sleepily when anyone addressed him, a pert sailor working with the British military mission, one of the waitresses from the Arachova whose hair, as she sat on my lap, would smell of mutton fat and cigarette smoke and who would fling her arms around my neck with a screech whenever the taxi bounced on a pot-hole; or a couple of girls in service ('hopeless from the start' as Cecil rightly prophesied, 'never take a couple') who would giggle alternatively as Götz tried to paw them and then refused his invitation to come into the house for a drink.

Sometimes it would be Cecil's evening, sometimes Götz's; sometimes, by a stroke of fortune, it would be the evening of both. 'You know, my dear,' Theo would say to me, 'if there's ever anything you want you've only got to tell me.'

'Thank you, Theo.'

'Meanwhile let me play you the tenth movement of my Concerto. You will see that I have made a number of alterations.' Running his hands up the piano, he would sigh and exclaim: 'Art, art, art! In the end—as Thomas Mann said to me in Venice—it's the only thing that *counts*.'

The Concerto was now occupying much of Theo's time; for he had, as he had prophesied, emerged from his 'depressive' phase and entered on a 'manic' one. The failure of the Fashion Parade was no longer mentioned; perhaps it had even been forgotten. Now we talked, not about Theo, the revolutionary designer of men's apparel, but about Theo, the composer; and instead of being consulted about whether I considered that two colours matched each other or lace would be preferable to net, I was asked to give my opinion on whether a certain theme should be given to the oboe or French horn. On both subjects I was, unfortunately, equally ill-informed; which may be the reason why Theo once burst out at me: 'Don't just say "H'm, h'm, h'm!" You have a mind—speak it.'

'But, Theo, I don't know.'

'I'm afraid you're lazy,' Theo said in a gently reproving tone. 'You left a lot of mistakes in Nadia's manuscript. Even *I* could see that.'

He had already decided that the first performance of the Concerto must be given abroad. 'Here I am surrounded by enemies—you saw what they did to me on that *never-to-be-forgotten-day*.' He was, I assumed, referring to the Fashion Parade. 'There is no one as jealous of the success of others as the Athenian; and no one as contemptuous of the products of his own country. But if I bring back laurels from London or New York or Vienna or Paris; then even Athens must accept me. . . . I think I would like, best of all, to have my first performance in London—in your Festival Hall—but whether I would want to play the solo, or conduct, or merely be a spectator, I have not yet decided. What do you think? You know how terribly I suffer from nerves.'

'I should advise you to be a spectator.'

'Yes, I feel you may be right—if only I can find a suitable pianist. You have some good pianists in England, haven't you? Solomon, and Dame Hess, and—what's his name?—Charlie Kunz. Do you think it would cost a lot to hire the Festival Hall?'

'A great deal, I'm afraid.'

'Perhaps Cecil would help me.'

A few days later Theo arrived, greatly excited, at Dino's flat, with a newspaper cutting which he removed from the lining of his hat: 'Look at this! It's about the arrival of Lady Aaronson.' He handed it to me and then snatched it back: 'Let me read it to you—you're too slow with Greek letters.'

It was the briefest of announcements: Lady Aaronson was expected in Athens the week after next, on a tour of the Greek schools which had benefited from the Fund of which she was President. Lady Aaronson and her husband, Sir Emmanuel Aaronson, the cutting went on, were generous patrons of the arts in England and it was due to their encouragement that the Frinton Festival of Modern Music had ever come into existence. Lady Aaronson would be a guest at the British Embassy.

'I must get on to the Ambassador at once. This is too good a chance to miss. If I can interest a woman like that —who has the whole of the artistic world at her feet— all my difficulties will vanish. Ah, if only the dear Princesse de Polignac were alive!'

'Funnily enough, I had a letter this morning about her.'

'About Winny de Polignac?'

'No, about Mabel Aaronson.'

'What!' Theo looked at me in amazement. 'You had a letter about her?'

'Yes, I was asked to take her round the sights. Still, if she's going to be at the Embassy, she probably won't need my help.'

'But we *must* take her around. . . . And I shall help you.' Theo looked into my face for a moment and then said: 'You're not joking, are you?'

'No, of course not. Why should I?'

'You have such an *odd* sense of humour. . . . But this is marvellous, Frank! Then you can introduce me, can't you?'

'Certainly, if you wish.'

'I suppose she *is* one of the most important people in the English musical world?'

'Oh, hardly that.'

'But she has a lot of influence?'

'A lot of money.'

'Which comes to the same thing. . . . And the family's very old, isn't it?'

'I don't know. . . . Mabel Aaronson was governess to two of my cousins.'

'Was *what*?'

'Governess.'

'Oh, how terrible! I think it's so tragic when girls of aristocratic families have to take jobs like that with people who probably made their money out of groceries. . . . Still, it seems all to have ended happily. She's very rich now?'

'Very, very rich.'

But like many people who are very, very rich, Mabel Aaronson was also very, very mean. She believed, as I remembered from the accounts of my cousins, in organised charity and not in spontaneous charitable acts; and just as, at my uncle's house, when a tramp called to beg, she would give him, not a shilling, but a coupon for the Salvation Army Shelter, so now, in Greece, the woman who had organised a Fund which had benefited schools throughout the country would hurry past, murmuring 'Disgraceful, this begging', when some ragged child attempted to extort the equivalent of threepence from her. However far across Athens we might be, she always insisted on returning to the Embassy for her meals: which might, I admit, be more charitably but less plausibly ascribed to her mania for cleanliness.

She was a tall, lean woman, with close-cropped sandy

hair streaked with grey the colour of pepper, a deter-minedly jutting chin under a vast nose, and great mascu-line hands and feet that never seemed to be properly joined to the attenuated arms and legs on which they moved. She always carried a string-bag which, soon after her arrival, was supplemented by another bag of supposedly Western Macedonian embroidery ('Perhaps your friend, Colonel Grecos, would be so good as to go in and buy it for me; when they see a foreign face, they always put up the price'). The sun had peeled her cheeks and given to the vee of her bony chest the inflamed texture of the badly plucked breast of a chicken. She was a woman of immense energy, intelligence and honesty. 'It's women like her,' the Ambassador's wife had remarked, 'who won the war for us.'

'And made it such hell for everyone else,' she then quickly added.

Lady Aaronson had been given the C.B.E. for her work with the Red Cross.

At the first meeting, it was obvious that she did not wholly trust Theo, and I ascribed this to a remark of his when we were driving past the Gymnastic Club in the taxi which Lady Aaronson would so obviously have preferred to have been a tram. 'What's that building?' she had asked.

'Ah—that!' Theo sighed. 'It's so many years since I set foot in there. Believe me, Lady Aaronson, you can get closer to Ancient Athens by walking in there for a minute than by spending a whole day on the Acropolis.'

'Are there some Classical remains there?' Lady Aaronson enquired.

'No, no—it's the Gymnastic Club. What happy days I spent there! There was a time when I and my dear friend, General von Freibusch, used to go there every morning before breakfast. But then there came a day when I realised that it was no longer compatible with my dignity to be seen hanging from the parallel bars or scrambling over a horse. And I never went there again.'

Lady Aaronson said nothing, but as she looked out of the taxi window her chin seemed to be jutting even more than usual and a vertical line had appeared between her sandy eyebrows. When, at the end of the afternoon, Theo left us, she asked:

'Tell me—who was that General von Freibusch that your friend mentioned? A German, I suppose.'

'Yes.'

'A Nazi?'

'It seems most unlikely.'

'Was he here during the Occupation?'

'No. He spent the Occupation in a concentration camp—until his death.'

'Oh.' Her face was clearing. But a moment later, she switched from a discussion of the ikons in the Benaki Museum to say: 'Did your friend say that his uncle had been a Minister under General Metaxas?'

'Yes.'

'He was a Fascist, surely—as far as I remember?'

'In a way—yes. But it was he who gave the famous "No" to Mussolini.'

'Oh, yes, of course—so he did! It's so difficult now to remember all that happened at the beginning of the war.

One was never quite sure who was on what side—one moment one was running a "Finland Fête" and the next moment a "Help Russia Bazaar".' Her large yellow teeth were revealed now in a smile. 'I liked your friend,' she said. 'He seems a real gentleman. . . . It was just that mention of a German General's name—one likes to get people's war records straight. . . . Still, I knew from the first that he was obviously all right. I'm usually pretty shrewd at seeing through people.'

Soon, Theo had completely won her over. She had, as I remembered from childhood visits to my cousins, an extraordinary greed for information which I myself was wholly incapable of satisfying. She would ask the measurements of the Theseum, the age of the Greek Queen and the exact number of members in Parliament; and invariably it was Theo, not I, who provided her with the answers. Often, I suspect, he was merely bluffing: but since there was no one at the Embassy likely to contradict her when, that evening at dinner, she announced that the pediment of the Acropolis weighed thirty-three tons, his position was safe. 'How knowledgeable the Colonel is!' she exclaimed when Theo had given her an entirely fictitious account of the Byron signature on the temple at Sunium. 'I suppose your work keeps you far too busy to get round much,' she added acidly to me.

Obviously she was no less charmed by Theo's exaggerated and, to me, slightly ridiculous gallantry and by the shameless way in which he would flatter her. Like many people who congratulate themselves on being able to 'see through' others, Mabel Aaronson never doubted the sincerity of any compliment that was paid to her.

Theo could tell her that she looked charming in her grey woollen two-piece and plaid skirt; he would compare her profile to that of a Hetaira in the Archaeological Museum; he would chuckle appreciatively when she barked out some roughly facetious comment, congratulate her on her knowledge and culture, and reiterate what a pleasure— what a real privilege—it was to accompany such a distinguished Englishwoman round his native city. Never for a moment did it seem to occur to her that he might not mean all he said.

It was on our third morning of sight-seeing that Theo first mentioned the subject of his music. He began to question Mabel Aaronson about the Frinton Festival, implying, as he did so, that for real music lovers it was Frinton, not Salzburg (which had become sadly disappointing) nor Edinburgh (which had always been vulgar) that exerted the most potent spell. 'How I have always wished to have enough money to take myself there! Last year I thought I had saved enough; but then I had a lot of unexpected demands from all sides, and in the end I had to content myself with a fortnight in Corfu.'

'Our beginnings are still small,' Mabel Aaronson said.

'But what does size matter?' Theo protested vehemently. 'That is what is wrong in modern life—this mania for size! Look at Mycenae! It might be a village!'

'True.'

Theo went on to ask if the works of foreign composers were ever performed; he meant, of course, he added, living foreign composers.

'No, not for the moment,' Mabel Aaronson said. 'We

113

really designed our Festival as a shop window for English talent only. But perhaps later . . .'

'Certainly, later,' Theo said.

As they parted he held her hand for an unusually long time after he had shaken it, and said: 'As one lover of music to another—may I ask something of you, Lady Aaronson?'

'Why, certainly, Colonel.'

'I have a few friends coming in to listen to some music of my own, next Thursday week—quite informal, you understand, the French Ambassador and his wife, perhaps Madame Venizelou, Nicholas Ghikas, Seferis—if he has returned from England—Spiro Harocopos and, of course, my very good friend, the Colossos of Maroussi—just a small, and very select, party. Won't you come too? I'd so like you to meet my little circle, and I am certain that they would like to meet you.' He smiled slyly: 'You probably didn't guess that I wrote music, did you?'

'No, I didn't. . . . What a surprise!'

'You will come, won't you? I'm going to play my Athens Concerto—but there'll be no orchestra, of course.'

'What day did you say? Next Thursday week? . . . Well, of course I must ask the Ambassador first. He's arranging my programme, and he really makes me work! Still, if he's willing to give me a few hours' leave, I'd be delighted to come.'

I had the feeling that, after she had spent two weeks at the Embassy, the Ambassador would be delighted to give her all the leave that she wanted.

'Wasn't that clever of me!' Theo said, as Lady Aaronson walked up the Embassy steps (as she had thanked us for taking her round, she had added: 'One day, when I'm not expected back to lunch here, you must let me take you both out to lunch at some little taverna round the corner').

'Very clever. But how are you going to get hold of all those guests you promised her?'

'Oh, it needn't be *exactly* those. Don't worry—I shall work on it. And you, of course, will help me. . . . Do you know the French Ambassador?'

'No.'

'No, I was afraid not. Do you know any Ambassadors?'

'Only our own. And Madame Landerlöst.'

'Who?'

I explained that this was the French wife of the Ambassador to one of the Scandinavian countries.

'Good. Well, you can get hold of her. And Spiro. And bring Dino, too. Oh, and contact some of those Council people in whose houses you're always drinking tea. . . . And, of course, there's the American crowd . . . But the most important thing is to get this Madame—Madame Whatever-she-is of yours. First things first; the rest will all follow.'

I was still terrified of Sophie Landerlöst, though by now I had become a frequent visitor at her house. She had once been on the stage, her friends saying that Landerlöst had first seen her at the Comédie Française, her enemies at the Bal Tabarin; though to me either alternative seemed equally improbable. She was a vast woman, with an enormous sagging dew-lap and bosoms that she was always patting as though they were footballs which she feared might slip out of position. Her feet and chubby, heavily be-ringed hands were tiny and so were her mouth and eyes. She dyed her hair a reddish purple, put green shadows on her eyes even during the day, and wore hats that seemed to be made entirely of sequins and ostrich feathers. One would not expect such a woman to be energetic: but Sophie Landerlöst, who climbed mountains, and swam and danced the Greek dances, was the most energetic woman I have ever come across. Landerlöst himself one seldom saw for more than a second; except that, when he spoke English, it sounded as if the water were running out of a bath, no clear recollection of him is now left with me.

Sophie and I first met in the bar of the Grande Bretagne. She was perched on a stool, and having obviously drunk too much, was engaged in trying to provoke a political argument with the taciturn bar-tender. She spoke Greek well: 'Plastiras — Papagos — Venizelos — Tsaldaris — Tsouderos—Markezinis—they are all ——': she used a French word which, if it had not been understood by the bar-tender, had certainly been understood by most of the other startled drinkers. Perhaps one of the gentlemen named was even then present. Again she repeated the word, and flung out her hand in which she was holding a black bag studded with gold stars. As neatly as if she had made an off-cut at cricket her glass of whisky jumped into my lap. 'Ah, pardon—pardon—pardon!' She began to mop me with an enormous silk scarf printed with Michelangelo's 'David', but in doing so, succeeded in spreading the damage further.

'It doesn't matter. It'll dry.'

'Yes, but what will people think until it dries?' She went off into boisterous laughter; and then crossed, swaying a little, towards a radiator. 'It's warm,' she said, patting the bars. 'Come and sit on it.'

I did not accept this invitation; but I accepted the drink which she next offered. We drank a lot together, and when we parted, though my trousers were dry, I myself was sodden.

'Do you swim?' she asked somewhat unexpectedly as I levered her into a taxi.

'Yes.'

'Good. Saturday next, twelve o'clock. Swim—then lunch.' It was like an order. 'Varkiza—you know Varkiza?'

'Yes.'

'Anyone can tell you how to find our villa.'

'But I have a lesson till one.'

'Come after your lesson then. . . . All right?'

'Thank you very much.'

'Good.' She said something to the driver, the taxi moved on, and I realised, simultaneously, that I still did not know her name. In the end I had to go back to the Grande Bretagne and ask the bar-man.

I arrived at Varkiza on Saturday in far from the best of tempers. I had had a two hour lesson with one of those tiresome students who always knew exactly what they wish, and do not wish, to learn (this one, a young man from the Foreign Service, was not interested in grammar but had an insatiable craving for idioms, which he invariably used wrongly) and I had then had to stand in a 'bus which was hot and crowded with people returning to their suburban homes for lunch. I had given up my seat to an old woman with a child in her arms and was furious that it had been taken instead by a plump young priest, carrying an umbrella. At Varkiza when I asked an old labourer for the Landerlöst villa, I was sent in the wrong direction.

'Is it far?'

'About one cigarette's walk.'

I could have consumed the best part of a packet by the time I found the path.

The villa was a bungalow, built in the Moorish style, with no pretence either to grandeur or attractiveness: Landerlöst never came here, and Sophie Landerlöst herself only came at the week-ends. When I arrived an oldish man-servant in a white jacket was laying a table out on the verandah and I saw that there were at least a dozen places. He glanced up as I descended the path, and then went on with his work.

'Madame Landerlöst?'

He answered, in French, that I would find the whole party down on the beach; he pointed at a path with the fork he held in his hand.

'May I change here?'

'Certainly, monsieur.'

I shivered slightly when I emerged, in my slip, into the spring sunshine, even though in the 'bus everyone had been sweating. As I began to walk down the path I realised that I had forgotten my glasses which I had taken off while changing, but I decided that it was not worth the trouble of going back to fetch them. I should not need them while I was swimming anyway.

Below me a number of people were splashing in the

water; though, from this distance, it was hard to tell which were rocks and which were people, and to decide whether I knew any of them or not. A voice shouted 'Hi'.

'Hi!'

Then another voice, which was Sophie's, shouted: 'What are you doing here?'

It was not a friendly question.

'You asked me,' I said.

'Did I?' Without my glasses and in nothing but my trunks, I felt curiously defenceless as I stood there above those anonymous upturned faces. 'When did I ask you?'

'In the Grande Bretagne Bar—last Monday.'

'I don't remember it. What is your name?' Slowly, with vast strides that sent the water streaming to left and right, she was wading towards me.

'Frank Cauldwell.'

'I've never heard the name.'

'We never told each other our names.'

'Then how did you discover mine?'

'From the bar-man.'

'He has no right to give people's names to strangers. . . . Anyway, now that you're here, you'd better come in. But take off your slip.'

'What?'

'Take off your slip!' I peered down in absolute amazement. 'Take it off!' she thundered.

Then I realised that as she stood before me with the water round her knees she was not wearing a pink bathing-costume, as I had short-sightedly imagined, but was in fact in the nude. There was nothing else for it: feeling even colder and more defenceless than ever I obeyed her command and scuttled, shame-facedly, into the water to join the equally shame-faced Embassy young men who were all in the same state as myself.

This was the woman whom Theo insisted that I should invite to the performance; the opportunity to do so presenting itself much sooner than I had expected. The day after Theo had been discussing his guests, Dino had driven me out into the country for a picnic; and as we passed the lower slopes of Mt Pendeli we saw ahead of us a large stationary green-and-cream American car with a C.D. plate behind it. A figure, chin supported by hand, was seated forlornly on a boulder by the roadside.

'Breakdown?' Dino suggested. 'We'd better stop.'

'It's Landerlöst,' I said. 'At least, I'm sure that's his car. And it looks like him.' Landerlöst was one of those people whose cars are easier to recognise than their faces.

'Can we be of any help? Are you in trouble?' Dino shouted.

The small figure rose and hurried towards us. 'No, thank you very much.' He peered into the car: 'Ah, it's Mr Cauldwell!'

'Good morning, Mr Landerlöst.' I introduced Dino.

'I've been sitting here since six,' he said gloomily. He was wearing breeches and a Norfolk jacket of hairy grey tweed and his long, thin, candle-coloured face looked snuffed out by the hat with a feather which he had pulled over his brow. 'My wife is there.' He pointed up the mountain.

'On the mountain?'

'Yes, the Mountaineering Club are presenting her with a medal. And apparently they do that on the top.' He added: 'We are supposed to be having breakfast down here. They said they would be back at eight, but now it is half-past eleven. You'll see the 'bus which brought the Club round the corner.'

'Did you drive yourself?' Dino enquired.

'No, we brought the chauffeur. He's also up the mountain. I, myself, don't like heights.' Yet again he glanced at his watch. 'I can't think what is keeping them.'

When ten minutes later the party appeared swaying and yodelling among the rocks and tufts of broom, it would have been obvious what had kept them even if we had not seen the wicker-covered flagons which most of the members of the Club were swinging from their hands. Sophie Landerlöst came first in a heavy pair of boots, ski-ing trousers and a leather wind-jacket, and as the stones crunched beneath her feet and the gorse made a scratching noise against her vast thighs, she never ceased to sing in a far from melodious baritone: 'Roll me over . . . in the clover . . . roll me over . . . and do it again . . .' Suddenly she caught sight of me, and pulling the scarf from her neck, she began to wave it in the air, shouting: 'Mr Cauldwell! Mr Cauldwell!'

I waved back.

'How nice to see you! And how nice to see you in your clothes! You look so much better in them—like most Englishmen.' I hoped that none of the members of the Mountaineering Club who were gathering round us would misunderstand; about Landerlöst I did not worry —somehow one never did.

121

'Come along, somebody! Give Mr Cauldwell a drink!' The mouth of one of the wicker flasks was pushed at me. I gulped and the raw ouzo burnt its way down. 'You must join our party,' Sophie cried out. 'We must celebrate this medal I've been given.'

I looked enquiringly at Dino: and Dino nodded to me with the faintest of grimaces. 'Really—Frank—your friends!' he would say to me afterwards.

We were all drunk when I at last mentioned Theo's performance. 'But I'd love to come! I'm mad about parties and I'm mad about music. . . . This wretched cook —he never hard-boils an egg properly.' Sophie began to mop at one of her footballs. 'Give me your handkerchief. . . . Yes, of course, I'll come. I've heard so much about your friend. I was told that he goes to the same corsetière as myself.'

I found it easier to believe that Theo went to a corsetière than that Sophie did.

Theo was gleeful when I told him of my success. He rubbed his bony hands on each other and said: 'Excellent, excellent, excellent.' Then he went to a cupboard and fetched down a tin of mint humbugs from which he offered me one. 'These were a present from a young English midshipman in the year after the war. I was of some—er—use to him in Athens.' I realised that I was being given what was in the nature of a reward.

'We now have eleven guests in all, and I aim to get twenty. With Madame Landerlöst already in the basket it shouldn't be hard to catch the other fish. You're a clever boy, Frank!' For a while he discussed how the other 'fish'

122

were to be caught, and then moved on to the subject of what refreshments should be provided.

'Götz will see to the tit-bits,' Theo said. 'Won't you, Götz?' Götz, who was busy darning one of Theo's socks, nodded his head. Two months ago I might have suggested that perhaps a caterer would do the job better; but by now I had learned that for all his apparent clumsiness and squalor Götz was an excellent cook and 'arranger'. 'But what about drink?' Theo continued. 'In the old days I always used to give my guests champagne. But that, alas—' he sighed—'is now out of the question.'

'Lady Aaronson is strictly teetotal,' I said.

'But our other guests must have something to drink.'

'Tea?' Götz suggested. 'Or coffee?'

'Sophie Landerlöst will be furious if she's brought here for a cup of tea or coffee. And so will most of the others,' I thought; then I said: 'I know; you'll have to make a Cup.'

'A Cup?'

'Yes, to people who don't drink a Cup always sounds quite innocent. They think it must be made out of lemonade and a dash of cider, with some cucumber and strawberries to give it a flavour. I'm sure Lady Aaronson would approve of a Cup.'

'Excellent idea! . . . I have a bottle of Cointreau I was given at Christmas, and that store-keeper from Ealing has promised me some more Naafi gin at his usual black-market price.'

Lady Aaronson was, as we had expected, the first to arrive. She was wearing a black woollen dress, with a single rope of pearls, pearl ear-studs and a gold brooch

123

that spelled out her name: 'Mabel'. I remembered that the last had been given to her one Christmas by my girl cousins at an age when they did not know better. ('Look at the jewellery,' Theo hissed at me. 'Perfect taste—discreet—no vulgarity. . . . That's what tradition does for you English.')

'Am I the first? I'm afraid I've arrived early.'

'On the contrary,' Theo said. 'The others are arriving late. It's a bad Athenian habit.'

Mabel Aaronson was wandering round the room, examining Theo's fantasiometric objets d'art with a mingling of astonishment and disapproval. Under her close-cropped sandy hair her face had been powdered white so that her freckles were obliterated; but her bare arms and the vee of her neck still looked as if they had been sprinkled with demerara sugar. 'What is all this?' she eventually enquired.

'This is my art,' Theo explained, hurrying up behind her. 'I call it fantasiometry.'

'What?' She used to use the same tone, I remembered, when, as children, she had caught us out in some improbable flight of imagination. She was blinking her eyelashes which were coated with powder, and drawing her mouth in tight. Fortunately, at the same moment, Götz and Cecil appeared.

'Ah, Lady Aaronson. Let me introduce two of my dearest friends to you. The Honourable Cecil Provender . . . and Freiherr Götz von Joachim.' Though I had frequently had to tell Theo not to call Cecil 'The Honourable', this was the first time I had ever heard Götz dignified by a title. They began to shake hands.

It was obvious that even apart from his nationality (I knew that Mabel Aaronson would already be sniffing out a 'war record' to 'get straight') Götz was unlikely to make a favourable impression on someone who, all her life, had set such an importance on the governess's virtues of cleanliness and tidiness; and it was no less obvious that Cecil, who could, when he wished, exert a wonderfully distinguished if patronising charm, would be a success.

'I believe you know my mother,' he started.

It was the perfect opening; for Lady Aaronson was one of those women who still think it charming when an unmarried man discusses his mother at length.

The woman whom Theo never called anything but 'my old girl' now came in with a plate of canapés in either shrivelled claw. She, a paralysed sister and a brother who worked at an undertaker's all lived together in a room which Theo had given them at the back of the house, and in return she was said to help with the rough work. But since, except on those occasions when Götz went round with a mop or a broom, the house was never cleaned, it was hard to discover what duties she performed. Tonight she had been asked to act as a waitress. She smiled at Lady Aaronson and gave a little nod of her head on top of its thin, chamois-leather neck; then, having put down the two plates, she held out a hand which Lady Aaronson, somewhat startled, took in her own. Muttering something in Greek, she perched herself on the arm of the chair in which I was sitting, crossed one bony leg over the other, and gave an excellent performance of following the conversation which Cecil and Lady Aaronson now resumed between them. Sometimes she would murmur

'Yes . . . yes . . . yes', and the wizened little head would shake up and down.

Suddenly Theo noticed her: 'Katina—I think you had better go and fry the Keftedes,' he said peremptorily.

She rose to her feet, and casting a number of backward glances at Cecil and Lady Aaronson, drifted from the room.

Lady Aaronson leant forward to whisper to me: 'Was that his wife?'

'No, not his wife. She lives here.'

'You mean that she's his . . .?'

'No, not even that. She's merely helping with the waiting.'

'How odd!'

Other guests had now begun to arrive. First there were two Australian girls about whom Theo, who always liked to spin myths about his friends, used to say that one painted with 'an El Greco-like intensity' and the other had 'all the qualities of a Virginia Woolf heroine'. They were jolly, large girls who were prepared to find anything in the old world amusing or interesting, and on this occasion they were wearing gym-shoes, slacks and sweaters. 'Quite Bohemian!' I heard Mabel Aaronson murmur to Cecil. There followed a small, bald American who, each time he shook hands round the room, said: 'Jake McClushen Junior of the United States Information Service. Pleased to meet you, sir'; Nadia Grecou who declared with great emphasis, 'I *know* it will be a success', as she picked out a few random chords at the piano and then seated herself in the most comfortable of the chairs where she began artfully to arrange her draperies; and a number of Embassy and British Council officials and their wives, Greek writers and painters, and members of the American Mission. Not a single composer or musician was present.

Theo, who was rapidly losing his head, all at once realised that no one had been given a drink. He rushed to Götz, and then to Cecil, and finally to me, hissing: 'Don't just sit there, for heaven's sake! Do be of use!'

'Certainly. What do you want me to do?'

But he had already shot off.

'Frank!' A moment later he was shouting to me across the room, an enormous earthenware pitcher held in both hands. 'Do come and help me! What's the matter with you? And where's my old girl?'

I began to take round glasses, most of which were examined dubiously by those to whom I gave them. Lady Aaronson sniffed at hers and asked: 'What's in here?'

'It's quite harmless—just a Cup,' I said.

'Ah, a Cup.' She sipped. 'H'm, it doesn't taste too bad. Quite refreshing. . . . Do open a window and let out some of this disgusting cigarette smoke.'

'I see that, like me, you don't believe in the use of stimulants, Lady Aaronson,' Nadia put in. 'Just some iced water for me, Mr Cauldwell.'

The small, bald American raised his glass and said in a voice that crackled like cellophane: 'Well, I'm sure we'd all like to drink to the success of our very good friend the Colonel's Concerto. When a man of over sixty—I think I am giving away no secrets there, indeed I hope I am not—can settle down to produce his first major musical work, then I think it says a lot both for his own vitality, and the vitality of his country, and indeed the vitality of the . . .'

His words were lost in the increasing uproar of conversation, but his mouth continued to open and shut.

After a few minutes, Theo came over: his face was red in patches, and his long, battered nose was shining with sweat. 'Where is your friend?' he demanded.

'Which friend?'

'Madame—Madame—Whatever-she-is.'

'How am I to know?'

'Shall I begin?'

'Give her five minutes.'

'Didn't you tell her what time she was expected?'

'Of course I did.'

'You ought to have told her that you'd fetch her.'

When Theo finally decided to begin the performance without Sophie Landerlöst, we had considerable difficulty in persuading the guests to sit down and stop chattering. Götz would shout 'Silence—silence—silence, please!'; Theo would clap his large, bony hands together and thunder out chords at the piano; I myself would wander round saying apologetically: 'I wonder if you'd mind sitting down now.' Until, at last, only Lady Aaronson could be heard whispering to Cecil: '. . . and, do you know, until I took charge, the heads of thirty-three and a half per cent of those unfortunate children were infested with lice . . .'

'The Athens Concerto,' Theo announced. He took a handkerchief and wiped the palms of his hands; then he fiddled with the piano stool, struck a chord, and once again fiddled. 'First Movement. *Marcia alla burlesca.*

Constitution Square.' Suddenly he got up, took down his beret which was hanging over a glass lustre on the mantelpiece, and put it on his head. He blew his nose noisily into a khaki handkerchief. Then he resettled himself: '*Marcia alla burlesca*,' he said.

The door opened.

'Are we terribly late? Goodness, how solemn we all look! . . . Hello, Mr Cauldwell! . . . You must be Colonel Grecos, aren't you? . . . Why, there's Mr McClushen— I never expected to see *you* here. And Dora Stratou . . . you must tell me all about your visit to Istanbul . . .' Behind Sophie there were four pink young men, in dark blue suits and blue-and-white striped shirts, who shifted in embarrassment from one leg to another, as she ran from guest to guest. 'I hope you don't mind, Colonel Grecos, but I brought some friends with me. This is Mr Annestedt who is from our own Embassy—' she pointed to one of the young men—'and this is Bobby, who is with the Americans—and Pierre, with the French—and this—this . . .'—she laughed. 'Well, I can't remember who and what this is. He's English, I think.'

Sophie lowered herself into the chair and I was about to sit at her feet when she hissed at me: 'Find me a drink!' I pretended not to hear, but she repeated: 'Mr Cauldwell, get me a drink.'

Theo swung round on the stool to watch me irritably as I creaked across the room, poured out a drink and then creaked back. He drew in a heavy breath, closed his eyes, and at last said: 'Well—shall we begin?'

Somebody cleared a throat; otherwise there was silence.

'*Marcia alla burlesca*. Constitution Square. . . . Drums
. . . flutes . . . violas and violoncellos . . .' For a while the
audience was amused by the extraordinary spectacle of
the old man in his beret, pounding at the keys, while he
shouted his directions. People exchanged glances, and
one of the Australian girls began to shake with giggles.
The other caught the infection from her, until they were
both shuddering soundlessly with handkerchiefs to their
mouths. Götz was leaning against the window, his eyes
closed; I noticed that he was wearing the Italian tie I had
given him when I was in hospital; it was the only time
I had seen him in a tie, and the knot was hanging just
above the second button of his shirt. He looked rapt, as
he had appeared before the ikon that day, seemingly so
long ago, when I had first seen him at Langada. Mr
McClushen was waving one hand, in which he held a
cigarette, in time to the music; the four young men
brought by Sophie were seated cross-legged on
cushions, their faces now crimson as they stared at the
rug before them. Nadia appeared to be sorting the
contents of her bag in her lap.

'*Adagio*. A night at the Argentina . . . Castanets . . .'
Theo clicked the fingers of his left hand together as he
thundered with the right. 'Piccolos . . .' He whistled and
then had to stop, because he wanted to sneeze. 'Tambourine . . .'

The door squeaked open and Katina's face appeared.
She began to tip-toe towards Theo and, stooping down,
whispered in his ear. He shook his head violently:
'Cymbals—boom—crash—boom!—cymbals—bam!—
bam!—bam! . . . Muted violins . . .' He began to hum

falsetto, swinging from side to side with an exaggeratedly sinuous movement of the shoulders.

Katina gave up; she came over to me. But I could hear nothing she said. 'Later,' I whispered. 'Later.'

Still she insisted on blowing into my ear; she was even plucking at my sleeve now, as she stooped above me. In exasperation I got up and followed her out.

'Yassou!' I was greeted in the back of the hall by an enormous Greek in uniform.

'Yassou,' I returned.

'Don't you remember me?'

I peered. 'Yes, I think so,' I said vaguely. We met so many people in uniform in our tours of the tavernas.

'Langada,' he said. 'I rescued you. Remember?'

'Yes, of course.'

'Harry—' I had never heard Cecil called this before— 'told me that if I ever got leave, I was to be certain to come and see him. I'm taking the boat to Crete tonight. I've only two hours—I dashed here from the station. Is he here?'

'Ye—es.'

'Where is he?'

'He's busy.'

'In there?' He pointed a massive thumb at the door from behind which Theo could be heard announcing: '*Andante*—the Lovers in the Zappeion . . .'

I nodded.

'What is it—music?'

'Yes.'

'Shall I go in?'

'No. I don't think you'd better. Come back later.'

131

'But I only have two hours.'

'Then it doesn't look as if you'll be able to see him.'

'I must see him. He told me that as soon as I was in Athens, I was to call. If you don't believe me, he wrote the address for me here——' He began to undo the flap of one of his breast pockets.

'I do believe you.' It was not in the least difficult to believe. 'But at the moment, he's busy.'

'What's he doing? Listening to that music?'

'Yes.'

'Well, surely, he can do that some other time.'

'No, you see . . .' I broke off; it was useless to try to explain.

'Look, I'll sit down here.' He lowered his enormous bulk on to a small Venetian chair, painted cream and gold, where he sat legs wide apart and hands dangling between legs. 'And you go in and say to him that Costa's here. That's all you need say. Costa from Crete. He'll understand.'

'But just at this moment I—I can't possibly——'

'Now you go and do that.'

I returned to the room, but I went back to my place without saying a word to Cecil. Sophie hissed: 'I bet you've been having a drink on the sly. . . . How long is this going to go on for?' By now everyone had a vaguely dazed, soporific look, except for the two Australians who were still choking and gulping tirelessly into their hand-kerchiefs while the tears streamed down their cheeks. Mabel Aaronson looked slightly different from the others; she, too, had the appearance of someone who had just been hit on the head, but from the oddly stiff way in which she held herself in her chair I suspected that in her case it was the unaccustomed alcohol, as well as the boredom, that was responsible for the change. She caught my eye, as I appraised her, and revealed her long, butter-coloured teeth in a bemused grin.

Suddenly the door opened again. 'Harry!' a deep voice hissed. 'Come here!'

Cecil looked up, startled; his head had been slowly nodding forward on to his chest, his eyes had been closed.

'Harry!'

Cecil got up and went out, while everyone exchanged glances. From outside one could hear the sounds of enthusiastic greetings in the demotic; Theo struck his octaves as if he were wishing to hurt them.

Ennui flooded back: Cecil was being unusually quiet, I thought. When Theo shouted 'Drums . . . drums . . . drums', I half expected, as on that other occasion, that there would come thuds from the other room. Inexorably, the sixth movement followed the fifth, and the seventh the sixth. Sophie Landerlöst began to creak on the broken springs of her chair. 'I'm parched!' she hissed. One of her young men had crossed his arms over his knees in a surreptitious attempt to glance at his watch; I, myself, had already glanced at mine and knew that an hour and a half had passed.

'Oh, Lord, how long, how long?' Sophie intoned softly, in time to the music. 'Stop him, stop him, for God's sake stop him!'

'How can I?'

'Well, I shall.'

133

I did not take this remark seriously and was amazed when, after a few bars of the movement which Theo called 'The Tavern Dancers', Sophie jumped to her feet. 'The *rebetiko*!' she exclaimed. She began to gyrate, clicking her fingers, in the small space between the audience and the piano. I had heard of her skill at these intricate dances; now it was being proved to me. Although she was so vast and her whole frame was supported on a pair of the flimsiest and highest high-heels I have ever seen outside Shepherd Market, yet there was an extraordinary grace and precision about the whole performance.

At first Theo played on, oblivious of what was happening; he was extremely hot and he called out his directions between gulps for air; his irregular face was red and swollen and glistening with sweat.

'Come on, somebody! Come and join me!' I drew back as Sophie put out an arm to me: unlike the unfortunate man to whom she next appealed, I did not work in her husband's embassy. 'Come along, Annestedt! If you don't know the steps, it's time that you learned them.'

The pink young man lumbered to his feet.

'And you!' Sophie cried, pointing at McClushen, who giggled and held both hands up to his face in a gesture of warding her off. 'And you!' she said to Dino.

Theo glanced over his shoulder, at last aware that the silence of his audience had been broken. But with a dogged persistence he continued to hammer out his music, right foot firmly pressing the loud pedal to the ground.

'Oh, but don't change the time!' Sophie shouted at

him, as he was moving into yet another of his sixty-nine themes. 'We're dancing a *syrto*, not a *slaviko*. Colonel Grecos, please! Some more of the *syrto*!'

'Yes, some more of the *syrto*!' echoed the people who were now stamping and stumbling about the floor.

There was a moment when Theo hesitated: and I wondered whether he would tell them to sit down, to shut up or to get out. But he had never been able to resist any opportunity to make others happy, even at his own expense; he had never been able to resist anything in the way of a 'party'; and he had never been able to resist the Greek dances which he alone, of the company then present, could perform better than Sophie Landerlöst. He paused, his bony hands held motionless for a second above the keys; conflicting emotions—pleasure and anger and disappointment and a kind of rueful self-mockery— passed in turn over his long, battered face. Then his hands descended; with a tremendous crash of octaves he had returned to the *syrto*.

Sophie Landerlöst let out an extraordinary bellow such as I had only heard before coming from the mouths of drunken dock-workers on Sunday nights in Peiraeus tavernas. Mabel Aaronson was cowering in her chair, watching the whole scene—she would, I was sure, describe it afterwards as 'an orgy'—with a fascinated horror.

'Come on, Mr Cauldwell! Don't be so lazy! ... And you there—you great hulking blond beast—' she flung out an arm at Götz who was hesitating between his loyalty to Theo and Theo's music and his obvious desire to gambol with so many, to him, attractive women—

'don't look at us as if you were a bull on the other side of the hedge! Come on!'

One dance followed on another. Dust rose from the floor and plaster fell from the ceiling. The drink had by now run out and two of Sophie's pink young men were sent off to buy some more. Theo had given up his place at the piano to Dino, who played far better, and was now persuaded to do a *hassapiko*—a dance which he performed better than any other—with Sophie as his partner. There were cheers as they finished.

Sophie announced that she must go to the 'lou', and returned a few minutes later, dragging Costa by one hand. 'See what I found there!' she announced. 'Isn't he wonderful? Look at his thighs! He says he comes from Crete and he's going to do one of the Cretan dances for us. Aren't you?' Costa, who was both embarrassed and delighted at being pulled into this strange gathering, put a vast hand to his face and giggled behind it.

Cecil appeared at the door which led into his bedroom: 'Costa! What are you doing here?'

'Come along, Mr Provender! We're having such fun. It's far too early for bed.'

Mabel Aaronson rose unsteadily to her feet.

'Goodnight, Colonel Grecos.' I felt sorry for her; she wanted to express scorn and disapproval, she wanted to leave on some cutting phrase. But all she could do was sway and wobble. She was still terribly drunk. 'Goodnight,' she repeated.

'I'll get a taxi for you,' I said.

When we reached the bottom of the outside staircase she looked back and saw the painted military policeman gleaming through the darkness. She started: 'And who is that?' she demanded thickly. 'What an extraordinary crowd of guests.'

'Well,' Theo sighed as the laughter and shouts of Sophie and her young men faded down the street, 'I think I can say that that was one of the most successful parties I have ever given. And there's still quite a lot of the drink left which those two boys fetched.' Götz was on his hands and knees picking up broken glasses: Cecil lay on the floor, supported by cushions, while he puffed at a cigar which McClushen had given him. 'Yes,' Theo sighed again, 'a most successful party. And I think, Cecil, that one can say that the greatest success of all was your friend from Langada. How magnificent he looked!'

'I hope he hasn't missed the boat.'

Suddenly Theo noticed that the pages of his score lay scattered around the piano stool and his face expressed first surprise; then, as recollection awoke, concern; and finally disappointment and anger. He began to mutter to himself as he picked up and sorted the sheets and at last exclaimed aloud: 'Fiasco! Again fiasco!'

'What did you say, my dear?' Cecil asked dreamily from his cloud of cigar smoke.

'I might as well throw all this down the lavatory.' But I noticed that he tenderly put the pages in a drawer, which he first had to unlock, and then locked again. 'And all because of that horrible, horrible prostitute! How dare she! What manners!'

'But it was a good party,' Cecil murmured. 'Wasn't it, Götz?'

'Yes, it was a good party,' Götz said with a heavy melancholy; he could never tell anything but the truth. 'A very good party. But poor Theo—what will become of the Concerto? Lady Aaronson was very angry, wasn't she?'

'Oh, damn Lady Aaronson!'

'That remark—if I may say so, Cecil—is typical of you. You don't care a jot that—that I've suffered this terrible set-back; that I've wasted so much money on this party; that—that the Concerto will obviously never be performed at Frinton.' Theo's lower lip trembled in a mingling of rage and grief.

Cecil blew a cloud of smoke into the air, his eyes half closed.

Theo turned on me: 'Why on earth you wanted to invite that woman I just can't think! You've travelled about a lot, you're no longer a child; and yet in some things you show a complete absence of any knowledge of the world. You must have guessed what would happen, didn't you? You must have known the sort of woman that she was! And why did you keep pouring drink down her throat?'

'*I* poured drink down her throat?' I asked in amazement.

'Well, wasn't it you who made all that noise getting her a drink just when I was starting? Really, you're too irresponsible! You're as much to blame as anyone for this utter, utter failure!'

'Now, look here, Theo, it was you yourself who said that you wanted Sophie Landerlöst——'

'That's right! Now put it all on me! And I suppose it was I who went out and told that wretched Cretan gendarme to come and call Cecil? . . . I'm not angry with you, but I really think the time has come for you to acquire a little savoir faire. Dino agrees with me.' When Theo wished to quarrel, he could usually name some absent friend in support of his accusations. 'Only yesterday he was saying that though, of course, in many ways you were a delightful guest, it was such a pity that you had never really learned——'

'Please leave Dino out of this!'

'Now don't fly off the handle. If I say these things, it's only for your own good. You've seen for yourself, this evening, the kind of havoc that can be caused by lack of consideration and an elementary tact. I've often wanted to talk to you about this; frankly, it's worried me a lot. It's not that I bear you any grudge—I know that you didn't *mean* any harm—but you must admit it's galling for me to lose a golden opportunity through the—the—well, I must call it stupidity—of a friend.'

'Really, Theo, don't be so ridiculous. You yourself need never have played those dances, need you? Why pick on me to——?'

'Yap-yap-yap-yap!' Cecil said dreamily. Again his cigar smoke curled upwards to the ceiling. 'Oh, pack it up, girls! Pack it up!'

The next day I was drinking at the bar of Zonar's when a large, bony hand came to rest on my shoulder. 'Well, my dear? How do you feel today?'

'Very well, thank you,' I replied stonily, without looking round.

'It's good to let off steam every now and then. You

tend to bottle everything up—like most English people. It's bad that, bad.' Theo perched himself on the stool next to mine. 'Please don't think I was in the least bit offended by all those things you said to me. When one loses one's temper, one always says things which one doesn't really mean. It takes a lot to offend me. So don't worry about it. I know you were feeling strung-up—and had also probably drunk a little too much, eh? Anyway it's all forgiven and forgotten. I never bear grudges. . . . But—' he grinned in the friendliest possible way—'as a punishment I shall make you buy me a drink. A gin-fizz please. A large gin-fizz and perhaps the smallest of small foie gras sandwiches.'

THE days that followed the performance of the Concerto were taken up with Cecil's return to Italy, my preparations for a summer holiday in England, and Theo's preparations for the tour he planned to make in Turkey.

Cecil, who had already spent far longer in Greece than he had intended ('Ever since I read the fourth book of the Greek Anthology at Eton, I felt it was the place for me,' he had said on one occasion) was the first of us to go. He left behind him a present of fifty pounds for Theo and a legacy of callers—sailors, navvies and evzones—who would appear at all hours at Theo's front door to ask if the English 'lordos' were at home. Sometimes the visitor would even be holding in one massive fist a crumpled piece of paper on which Cecil had written his name and address.

My own preparations before starting for England consisted chiefly in trying to collect the small sums of money that were owing to me for lessons: but since most of my students were themselves planning to visit what they called 'Europe', this task was not easy. Theo's preparations were on a far more elaborate scale. These days his room was piled with guide books and brochures and photographs while, with the help of maps which he was incompetent at folding and usually left lying open on the floor, he would work at his innumerable itineraries. Should any visitor ever be foolish enough to mention that he had ever known anyone who had any connection with Turkey, Theo would insist that he should sit down at once and pen a letter of introduction.

'And what about you, Götz?' I asked one afternoon, when I found myself alone with the German. 'Will you be going to Turkey or returning to Germany?'

'I don't know.' Götz was sewing on to the back of Theo's tall grey felt hat a roll of canvas which could be drawn up or let down at will by the pulling of a cord; it was Theo's own idea, to protect, as he declared, the back of his neck from the violence of the Turkish sun. 'I had a letter yesterday from my father—my first for over a year—asking me to go back. He's getting old and his sight is bad. I think he is willing to forget and forgive everything; that is the impression I have.'

I am naturally inquisitive, and my years in Greece where everyone asks personal questions, have made me even more so. 'What has he got to forget and forgive?' I asked.

Götz rammed his needle through the thick felt. 'Oh, I don't know,' he said. 'I haven't been the ideal son. I was never any good at the University and the Army rejected me. Then I had trouble with a girl and he had to pay her off.' He blushed deeply and his harelip quivered, as it always did at times of embarrassment or emotion. Blinking his short pink eyelashes, he added: 'Besides, I never had any interest in the business. I wanted to travel.'

142

'What business is it?'

'I don't know how you call it. We sell things like kettles and pans and nails and paraffin.'

'Hardware.'

'I think my father would like me to take it over from him. It's a good business,' he added.

'And would you like to take it over?'

Götz raised his head from his sewing and looked at me with his sad, brooding eyes. 'No,' he said at last. 'It would be death.'

'But don't you think, if your father is willing to have a reconciliation, that you ought to do what he asks?'

'It might be wiser,' Götz agreed. As he again pushed the needle into the felt, I noticed that his forefinger was encrusted with a rim of blood where he had savagely bitten the nail. 'But then—' he sighed—'there's always Theo.'

'Theo?'

'He can't go alone to Turkey, can he?'

I looked dubious.

'He's going to stay at the Embassy,' I said at last.

'Only for a few days. And even that may not be true. You know how he—he *imagines* things.' Götz brought out these last words almost as if he were afraid that he was being guilty of a disloyalty to Theo in saying them at all. 'He wants to visit all the old Greek cities on the Asia Minor coast—Troy and Pergamum and Ephesus—and he's really too old to do that sort of thing alone. Isn't he?'

'But, Götz, you must think of yourself. After all, if this is your chance to put things right with your family. . . .'

'Yes, I know, I know. And I'd like to see them again. I quarrel with my father, but I'm fond of him, I think. And I'm very fond of my mother. And only last night— it was so hot that I couldn't go to sleep—I began to think of Germany and how nice it would be to return there and find everything so green and fresh after the dust and dryness here. I *want* to go back. Not for ever, of course, but just for a few weeks. But I don't see how I can. After all, Theo's been so good to me, hasn't he? I owe him so much. And it would be sad if this visit which he's been so much looking forward to should now get spoiled.'

Although after this I doubted if I should interfere any further, I made a half-hearted attempt to hint my feelings to Theo when we next discussed the trip.

'Is Götz going to accompany you?' I asked.

'Naturally.'

'Then he won't be returning to Germany?'

'Why should he? You know how he hates his home.'

'Yes, but it's nearly three years since he was last there, isn't it? He must want to go back some time. I should have thought this was a good opportunity for him. He always says that he can't bear the heat anyway. Do you want him all that much?'

'Frank, Frank, Frank!' Theo was playfully reproving. 'I know what you're thinking, you horrid little snob! You're imagining that they're going to look down their noses at him at the Embassy. Well—let them! If they want me to stay, they must put up with Götz too. And if they don't like it, there are always hotels: not very good hotels, so I hear, but dirt and bugs have never worried me. No, Frank. If you think that I'm going to push Götz off to Germany, because he's not what is considered "acceptable" in the eyes of the beau monde, you're very much mistaken. It would be a thoroughly disloyal thing. Appearances may, at the first glance, tend to be against him, but what do appearances matter? The boy has a heart of gold. Eighteen carat.'

I said nothing more: but I wondered, perhaps cynically, if this passionate defence of Götz and, by inference, attack on myself were a genuine outburst of feeling or merely a clever side-stepping of an issue which Theo selfishly would not face. One could never be certain; Theo had, after all, always been more successful at deceiving himself than his friends.

Cecil's gift of fifty pounds was now being recklessly spent on equipment for the journey. I remember a folding canvas bath one of the struts of which was broken by Götz when he hoisted his massive buttocks into its flimsy structure; an insecticide so potent that, squirted in Theo's sitting-room, it gave us all hay fever; a pair of boots which had the appearance of being lined with sponge; a portable pressure cooker, capable of reducing potatoes to pulp within five minutes, during all of which time it emitted a shrill whistle; and innumerable small gadgets, items of clothing and note-books of all shapes and sizes.

One afternoon Theo arrived at Dino's flat, where I was still staying. I was in the middle of a lesson, but since he had sent a message by the servant that the matter was urgent, I went out to see him.

'So sorry to worry you, my dear, in the middle of your irregular verbs, but I must have your advice. I've just remembered that I've forgotten a most important item. . . . Ties!'

'Ties!'

'I must have some ties. Some new ties.' He touched mine. 'That's a pretty one. And I like the one that you gave to Götz when you were in hospital.' I wondered if this were a hint that I should also give one to him. 'You have such good taste in ties. Won't you come out with me and help me to buy some?'

'But I have a lesson now.'

'I can wait.' Theo walked over to Dino's desk and picked up a letter. 'This is from the Lord Chamberlain. Does Dino know him?'

'I suppose so. I don't know.'

'Such a "parvenu"! . . . I shall be quite happy here.' He sat at the desk. 'You go back to your student and I'll wait for you to finish.' He was already reading the letter.

We went to one of the large multiple stores where artificial ties could be bought for the price of real silk ties in Italy. 'You have such exquisite taste, my dear,' Theo murmured, returning the ties I had chosen back to the shop-girl. 'Now *that* is rather fetching.' He held up a swirl of liver, cucumber and carrot and then put it against my jacket. 'One notices the influence of our transatlantic cousins, of course. But it's discreet. It catches the eye. What do you think?'

'Frankly, Theo, I think it quite hideous.'

Theo put it on one side; he intended to buy it.

Soon he had accumulated half a dozen such monstrosities, his favourite bearing the face of a woman, pink on a black ground, with the inscription 'Je cherche un homme'. He giggled as we left the shop and slipped his arm through mine: 'Now I'm really set up. Do you know, I haven't bought a new tie since I visited Paris in nineteen-thirty-seven?'

When we reached home, he unwrapped his parcel and again examined the ties. 'I shall give you this one,' he said, holding up the fantasy of liver, cucumber and carrot, 'as you've been so patient with me all this afternoon.'

'No, really, Theo. Keep it, please.'

'Perhaps you'd prefer one of the others?'

I was not sure, as so often, whether he was joking at my expense.

'I have so many ties—far too many.'

'As you wish.'

He had fetched a sewing basket from the cupboard and, going into his bedroom, he returned trailing a number of tattered and soiled ties which he set beside the new ones. He took up a pair of scissors and began to pick at the one he had offered me. I watched him in bewildered silence.

All at once, he looked up and smiled at me with an extraordinary cunning. 'I recommend this dodge to you,' he said, inserting the point of the scissors into one of the old ties.

'What are you doing?'

He held up a label. 'Charvet,' he said. He held up another: 'Sulka.' Another: 'Turnbull and Asser.' Then, with tremendous contempt, he picked up the label of the Athens multiple store between finger and thumb, as though it were a used surgical dressing, and threw it into the fireplace. 'Servants are such snobs,' he said. 'When one's valeted at an Embassy, a Charvet label makes all the difference.'

He continued to unpick and sew.

Suddenly Götz ran in: he was breathless, his face was green and clammy, and his hair fell in an irregular fringe over his eyes. One of the shoe-laces of his gym-shoes was flapping loose, his shirt had worked out of his trousers at the back. 'Ah, there you are!' he gasped. 'I went down to Dino's, and then I came back here, and then I went down there again. I've been looking for you everywhere.' His powerful chest was heaving for breath.

'What is it?' Theo demanded.

'It's Nadia . . . They've just telephoned from the Red Cross hospital. She's had a terrible accident. You must go there at once. They've been trying to trace you for hours.'

Theo dropped the tie with its smudged woman's face, the 'Turnbull and Asser' label trailing a needle, and rose, trembling and white, to go towards Götz. The German put out an arm and Theo clutched it with both hands. 'Is she . . . really ill?' he asked.

'Very ill.'

'Come with me, come with me,' Theo said, first to Götz and then myself.

While we were driving in the taxi to the Red Cross hospital, he kept asking Götz: 'But how did it happen? Where did it happen?' and Götz would answer patiently: 'Theo, I don't know. They didn't tell me.' As he put these questions, in a kind of bewildered stupor, Theo never ceased to stroke the warts on his lean face with the tips of the fingers of his right hand.

Nadia had come round from the anaesthetic and, though obviously in considerable pain, she was able to talk. She lay on her back, with one leg and an arm supported in the air; her nose looking extraordinarily long and sharp and pink as it poked up through the voluminous bandages wound all about her.

Theo ran to her bedside: 'How are you? Are you all right, Nadia?'

'I'm quite all right,' she said, with a kind of obstinate petulance. 'But they insisted on giving me some kind of dope which has made me feel odd and dreamy. I'm quite all right,' she repeated, as though stretching her will to its agonised utmost. 'Why make all this fuss? . . . Oh, do stop wringing your hands like that, Theo. You look so absurd. You'd better go; I want to go to sleep.'

We led Theo off, and we and the doctors and the nurses all told him that Nadia would be all right. I certainly believed it, though later the surgeon said, as though to excuse himself: 'We knew all along that she hadn't a chance in a thousand.'

The next time we went to visit her complications had set in and she was running a high fever. Theo saw her first, while I waited outside with Götz; then he shambled out and told me: 'She wants you, Frank. She says she must see you.'

I went in, feeling oddly terrified, and she whispered: 'Is that you, Mr Cauldwell?' Her eyes glittered sideways at me from under the bandage.

'Yes.'

'Good. Now listen.' Even at this moment her voice carried its quiet authority. 'Sit down.' I sat. 'Can you hear me?'

'Yes, Mrs Grecou.'

'Good. . . . I want to talk to you about my play. In case anything should happen to me. I shall get better. But in case anything should happen to me. You understand?'

'Yes, Mrs Grecou.'

'I leave it to you. I make you my literary executor. You must prepare it for the B.B.C. and see that they perform it in . . . in a suitable fashion. I trust you for that.'

'Yes, Mrs Grecou.'

'Of course this is only if something should . . . should happen to me. But I shall get better. I know I shall get better.'

Theo had slipped in and he now came to the bed and squatted beside it, his knee joints creaking noisily as he lowered himself. More than ever now, his face seemed to have the colour and texture of gruyère cheese, as he looked at Nadia in an agonised sharing of her suffering.

Suddenly her eyes caught him: 'Don't look at me like that!' she hissed. 'I know what you're thinking. How do you expect me to get well, when you surround me with these terrible thoughts of yours?' Theo was continuing to stare at her with the same aching pity. 'No, don't look at me, don't look at me! I forbid you to look at me! If only you had never held the thought that something like this might happen to me. It was your wrong thinking!

It was your fault! Don't look at me! Don't even think about me! Don't think about me! Don't think about me! I forbid you to think about me!'

But to think about Nadia was, unfortunately, something that Theo could never stop doing.

In Greece they bury people quickly and Nadia was buried on the morning after her death.

We returned, Götz and I, to the house with poor Theo. There seemed, as always on such occasions, nothing to be said that would not sound either insincerely pious or trite or trivial: so we said nothing at all. I do not think I was much comfort to Theo, but Götz obviously was: merely by putting a hand on the German's shoulder or taking his arm, Theo seemed to derive the kind of consolation that children derive from curling up in the lap of a grown-up whom they love. 'Dear Götz,' he murmured once, removing between finger and thumb a hair that lay, platinum in the sunlight, on the German's frayed and shiny blue suit. He made a small 'T't, t't' noise. Then he asked: 'Are you frightened of death, Frank?'

'Yes.'

'And you, Götz?'

'Yes.'

'I wonder if there is anyone who isn't.'

When we got home, Götz settled Theo in the best armchair, as though he were an invalid, and put a rug over his knees. 'Now I shall make some tea,' he said. 'And you stay here and talk to Frank, will you?'

But Theo was in no mood to talk. His hands clasped,

the thumb and forefinger of the right ceaselessly turning the ring on the little finger of the left, he stared at the fireplace in which were still lying the pips and skin of the orange of which he made his breakfast. 'Ah, yes . . . yes . . . yes . . .' From time to time he would sigh out that characteristic phrase, and his head would be shaken from side to side.

Suddenly, he rose to his feet, letting the rug slip to the floor.

'Can I fetch you something?'

He ignored me. Going to a cupboard, he began pulling out an extraordinary collection of haphazard objects—letters, and tattered bits of cloth, a broken vase, a recorder, a draughts board, a bird-cage—which he flung irritably on to the floor regardless of whether they would smash there or not.

'What are you looking for?'

'This.' He held up a glass jar, vast enough to contain sweets in a village store in England, which still carried the label 'Bath Salts. Blue Grass'. 'She always used these,' he said.

He put the jar on his desk, and then going from drawer to drawer, cupboard to cupboard, room to room, repeatedly loped back with something to add to it. He fetched a button off a Tsarist uniform; a strip of grey chiffon, perhaps that same material Nadia had worn when I first met her; a crushed orchid ('I found it in the Crimea') removed gently from between the pages of a book on botany; a glove stretcher; a buff for the nails; a piece of Turkish delight ('She gave me the box for Christmas'); the cover of a number of the *Christian Science Journal* . . .

Götz brought in the tea, and twice we called Theo: 'Your tea will get cold.'

Theo did not answer; he did not even appear to hear us. Slowly, fragment by fragment, he was building up one of his 'objects' inside the glass jar.

Götz went over to him; he put a hand on his shoulder, and said gently: 'Theo, what are you doing? Please drink your tea.'

Absorbed, Theo took up a pair of scissors and began to cut the cover of the *Christian Science Journal* into a woman's face. 'Proust was right,' he said. He held up the paper and examined it; then he gave another snip. 'I remember once he said to me in Bruges: "Theo," he said, "it is Art—not Time—that heals all wounds."'

8

I RETURNED to Athens to find a change in both Theo and Götz. Physically, they were thinner and the sun which had burned Theo's usually yellow face to the colour and texture of a pomegranate, had so peeled Götz's nose and cheeks that it looked as if he were in the first stages of lupus. But, in Theo's case, the change was not only physical. He seemed to suffer from increasing periods of despondency when he did not wish to go out or to read or to talk or to thump at his piano, but only to sit, turning his signet ring and staring at the fire-place. In the past he had prosecuted all his various feuds with disapproving relatives, friends who had 'let him down' and 'jealous' fellow artists, with a vigorous acerbity. But now he was strangely softened. If he wished to take me to task for some imagined slight, he would not, as once, lash out at me with sarcasm and abuse, but instead he would gently and sorrowfully show how deep had been the wound that I, in my thoughtlessness, had inflicted on a man who was too old and tired to rise to defend himself. This new attitude—as he probably knew—made me feel far worse than the old one.

Financially, with Nadia's death, he was now better off, and instead of merely looking into the bars when he did his evening tour, he could now afford to sit down and buy himself, and sometimes even his friends, a glass of ouzo or of cognac. Yet this tour, which once he would insist on making even when he was suffering from neuralgia or rheumatism or influenza, now seemed to have lost for him most of its interest. If at seven he put his beret on his head, knotted his scarf and demanded: 'Well, how about a stroll?' one felt it was habit, not inclination, that was drawing him from his chair. 'Your friend seems vastly improved,' Dino remarked. But I was apprehensive; I was not at all sure that this was, in fact, an improvement.

Götz had once again become infatuated soon after I returned; and Theo who, in the past, had always been indulgent to these agonised enthusiasms, was now either indifferent, morose or openly scornful when the subject was mentioned. We had first seen the girl when we had gone to swim from a beach a few miles from Athens, opposite the coast of Euboea. Götz had 'discovered' this beach for himself two years previously, and whenever we went swimming, whether to Vouliagmeni or Varkiza or Phaleron, he would always exclaim: 'Ah, but this is nothing compared to *my* beach. It's vonderful there! Fantastic!' Theo (who only paddled) would then pick a shred of sea-weed from between his long toes and say: 'I don't believe this beach of yours exists.'

'But of course it exists! I shall take you there. . . . The only thing is, there aren't any buses.'

One day we decided to go on bicycles which we hired from a shop next to Theo's house. 'Let me have one without a bar,' Theo said. 'At my age it's so much easier to mount.' He was wearing knickerbockers, some canary yellow stockings and a blouse which made a large balloon between his shoulder-blades as he pedalled off. Götz had an enormous rucksack beneath which he crouched, his vast blond thighs, naked in the abbreviated shorts he was wearing, thrusting like pistons beside me. 'But this is wonderful!' Theo cried. All his melancholy seemed to have gone. 'Why did we never think of this before?' He tinkled his bell joyously as he wove through some pedestrians. 'Why didn't you tell me what fun biking was? I love this! How easily one moves! What grace! What smoothness!'

But soon he was grumbling, as his face broke out into red patches, sweat began to darken the blouse under his arms, and his breath came whistling from between clenched teeth. Götz had said that it was a mere eleven kilometres; that the road would be excellent; that the wind would be behind us for the whole journey (he all but promised that the wind would change to be behind us for the whole journey back). But it was now obvious that either his memory had been at fault or that conditions must have altered greatly since his last visit. Often we had to dismount; and when we did not dismount, we had to bump over stones and ruts, or pedal frantically to extricate our wheels from mud that was as sticky as melted chocolate. 'It's unfortunate it rained yesterday,' Götz remarked.

'It's even more unfortunate that your memory is so bad.'

'But it wasn't like this when I last came.'

'I know that Greece is falling to pieces pretty rapidly,

but I can't believe that that asphalt road you were talking about can have become *this* in the space of two years.' Theo hit a large stone and swallowed the last two words as his bicycle reared upwards like a horse. 'Oh——' he shouted, using what he defended as 'a decent Anglo-Saxon expletive' when we reproached him for his language.

'Patience, patience!' Götz said. 'Look at that view. It was worth coming for that alone.' A jeep at that moment passed us, and the dust swirled up, to fill our eyes and mouths and noses.

Coughing and spitting, Theo said viciously: 'Charming, absolutely charming. Charming view!'

'Wait till you see the beach.'

When we did at last see the beach, looking down at it from where the road plunged precipitously into a gully filled with rocks the size of a man's head, we each of us gave an independent gasp of horror. Even the beach at Phaleron could not, at that moment, have been more crowded.

'This *is* your beach, isn't it?' Theo asked.

Götz could easily have told a lie; there were, after all, innumerable beaches empty on either side. But lies had never come easy to him: 'Yes,' he said, going slowly crimson. 'It looks as if someone else must have discovered it.'

'Someone else!' Theo gave a harsh, croaking laugh.

I tried to appease him by some remark about the gregariousness of Greeks. 'It's really an advantage, because those of us who like solitude can always find it. Let's go on a little.'

'And push this bloody bike! I'm going to leave it here.'
Theo dropped the bicycle with a clatter into the gully.

'Take care! If it's damaged, we shall have to pay for it,'
Götz warned. 'You can't leave it there, anyway. Someone will steal it.'

'They're welcome.'

Eventually Götz himself retrieved the bicycle and
pushed it along with one hand while he pushed his own
with the other. 'We'd better leave them all at that cottage
over there,' he said.

There was a young man sitting in the sun outside the
cottage, while a cat and a child of indeterminate sex
scrabbled together in the dust at his bare feet. He took the
bicycles from us and then, with the usual insatiable
curiosity of the Greeks, asked if we were American.

'No,' Theo said. 'Japanese.'

'Japanese?' His small eyes widened in his sunburnt
face. 'But that's a long way away, isn't it?'

Theo shrugged his shoulders. 'Far enough. We came by
airship,' he added.

'By what?'

'Airship.'

'Oh.' The young man had now begun to look alarmed.
'And what are you doing here?'

Theo put a finger to his lips: 'Sh!'

I had begun to giggle at this childish deception and,
to hide my giggles, was playing with the cat. Theo
pointed: 'In Japan we worship cats.'

'Oh.' The young man seemed no longer capable of
saying anything else.

'Cats are holy. We think they have souls.'

'Oh, come on, Theo,' I said.

'My friend doesn't like me to talk about religion to strangers. . . . Goodbye—thank you so much.' Then, as we walked off, he exclaimed: 'Fool, incredulous fool! That's the Greek peasant! Will believe anything!' In the past he had always praised the Greek peasant for his gaiety and courage and natural intelligence and it was sad now to hear the rasping scorn with which he spoke these words.

Suddenly the youth was shouting above us, his hands cupped to his mouth.

'What does he say?' Theo demanded, halting.

'He says something about a shark,' I answered.

'A *what*?'

'A shark. At least, I think that's the Greek word for a shark.'

Theo shouted back: 'What did you say?' He listened, and then turned to us appalled. 'Did you hear that? He says that two years ago a girl was eaten by a shark when bathing from this beach. We'd better not go.'

'Oh, nonsense, Theo!' Götz protested.

'He's obviously getting his own back on you for having pulled his leg,' I added.

'Besides, a shark doesn't stay in the same place for two years,' Götz said.

Theo shook his head from side to side and tightened the knot of his scarf: 'I don't like it.'

Götz had already begun to race down the path that zig-zagged between rocks and stunted wind-blown olive trees and I followed with Theo behind me. 'Come on!' Götz yelled. 'It's vonderful! And no one in sight!'

It was one of those long, golden, deserted beaches which, miraculously, one can find even ten miles from Athens. 'I'm hot,' Götz said. He threw off his rucksack and then began to wrestle with his sweat-shirt which he had tugged over his head; he always gave the appearance of having been poured into his clothes hot, and to get himself out of them was like peeling an orange. Soon he was standing before us naked.

Theo, perched on a rock, stared at him with a morose admiration. 'Aren't you going to put on your bathing trunks?'

'Why should I? There's no one about.'

'Are you really going to bathe?'

'Of course.'

'And you, Frank?' I, too, had begun to throw off my clothes; after the heat and dust of the journey it was wonderful to feel the breeze cool on my naked skin.

'Yes, I shall bathe.'

'It seems to me most unwise.'

'But why, Theo?'

'Most unwise,' he repeated. He looked from one of us to the other and then said: 'You look like Homeric heroes.' He was not being ironical, of that I am sure: and I glanced at my own body and then at Götz's in silent amazement.

'Now get your shoes and stockings off,' Götz said, like a nanny to a peevish child, 'and have a good paddle.'

'Certainly not! I've no intention of going near that water. With that—that *monster* about, it's most inadvisable.' We both began to laugh, but Theo reproved us angrily: 'That's right—laugh if you wish. But let me tell you that only last year the cousin of a very dear friend of mine in Corfu was eaten by a shark with *hundreds* of people around her.'

'But no shark is going to come as far in as where you paddle.'

'I shall have a nap,' Theo said. 'But please—please, I beg of you—don't go too far out.'

Theo did not sleep: he sat on his rock, his hands clasped together, and watched us as we raced, and splashed, and attempted to duck each other. He looked curiously forlorn and old as we looked back at him from the water, his green beret and his yellow stockings and his plum-coloured shirt all seeming to melt back into the landscape of multi-coloured rocks, sand and olive trees that was now quivering in the midday heat. One felt that, if he stayed there long, all that was Theo would be absorbed and nothing would be left for us.

As we came out of the water, he exclaimed: 'Thank God—you're safe!' I had failed to take his anxiety with any seriousness, but now the tone of these words and his obvious and touching relief made me realise that he had genuinely feared for us. Götz, too, must have made the same surprised discovery for, all wet as he was, he went and got on the rock beside Theo and put a long, stringy arm about his shoulder. 'There, Theo,' he said. 'Your chicks are home safely.'

From that moment Theo's petulance and moroseness passed. As he munched a sandwich he began to sing

> 'It was the good ship *Venus*,
> My God, you should have seen us . . .'

in his still vigorous baritone.

'Where on earth did you learn that, Theo?' I asked.

'Oh, from one of the boys,' he replied. 'I learned a lot from your British tommies,' he added with an outrageous wink. 'Come on, Götz—fill up our glasses.

> 'The captain had a daughter,
> She fell into the water . . .'

Götz, who had a strain of prudishness in him, protested: 'Theo—please, please, please! Why do you want to spoil all these vonderful things around us with a disgusting song like that?'

Theo replied by cracking his hard-boiled egg on the back of Götz's head.

Looking back now, I realise those were some of the happiest hours I spent in Greece: and yet it would be hard to say why. There had been other picnics by the sea; on other days we had eaten and drunk as well, the water had been as beautiful, and each of us had been in an equally cheerful mood. Yet it is this occasion, and not all those others, which now comes back to me with a terrible, choking force, as I crouch over a gas-fire.

We dozed, and bathed again, and then dozed once more. Theo collected some shells, tying them up in a handkerchief which he then forgot and left under an olive tree. Götz put a crab on my chest while I lay with my eyes closed: a practical joke of a kind that I have always found hard to appreciate. He even croaked part of Isolde's narration in his unmusical bass, making Theo sigh, again without irony: 'Ah, you Germans—so musical, so musical.' Then, regretfully, we packed the rucksack and began to climb the hill.

The young man was still where we had left him, lolling on his chair. He smiled sleepily and, tugging with his bare, prehensile toes at a tuft of grass before him, offered us a glass of wine. It was from his own vineyard, and he was delighted when we expressed our appreciation of its harsh, ringing flavour. We all felt a little ashamed of Theo's deception earlier in the day.

The wine made us drowsy and at the first village at which we arrived we got off our bicycles at a café where the tables straggled on to the road, and ordered ourselves some coffee. It was that hour, just before sunset, when on Sundays Mediterranean people drift up and down a crowded main street or water-front to take the evening 'volta'. The village at which we had stopped had a main street of less than two hundred yards, and that two hundred yards must at that moment have held all its inhabitants. They walked, arm in arm and girls separate from boys, slowly up and down, in a cloud of dust that had already made an iridescent sheen on the tops of our cups of coffee. The boys wore dark grey or dark blue suits, the girls dresses of purple or orange or mauve or lemon-yellow or bile-green, which in a light less dazzling would have been horrible in their clashings with each other. Sometimes a car or a bicycle would slowly make its way between the thronged strollers who would part reluctantly to either side of the thoroughfare.

'What a curious custom,' I said. 'Do you suppose we'd do it in England if the weather were better?'

'You would, if that was the only way you could see a girl,' Theo replied.

'Look!' Götz exclaimed excitedly; he had been watching the crowds.

'At what?'

'There!' His hand gripped my arm. 'She's fantastic.'

'Who?' The effect of so many faces passing and repassing had been that I could no longer distinguish one from another.

'She's gone now. But I think that she saw me.'

It seemed to me not unlikely; we were sufficiently conspicuous for everyone who passed to examine us with that curiosity which Greeks never feel it impolite to show.

'There!' Once again Götz clutched my arm; next morning, when I took my bath, I would find two bruises.

She was certainly a girl of more than usual charm, with her dark hair falling smoothly from a centre parting, her long, smooth brown legs with their childish ankle-socks and flat-heeled strap-shoes, and her small, slightly pert face in which the eyes lay oblique and large and glistening. She was sixteen, I guessed, and she had that air of precocious maturity which is at once the most attractive and most touching feature of peasant girls of her age. She was walking arms linked on either side with two other girls, one fat and one thin, who were certainly not her equals in charm, and all of them were giggling, with their eyes lowered, as they swayed past our table.

'Vonderful!' Götz said.

'What is it, Götz?' Theo asked irritably, as he attempted to fish some unidentifiable object—a fly or a piece of grit —out of his coffee.

'That girl!'

'Girls, girls, girls. You think of nothing else.'

'Look, she's going to pass us again! She's deliberately going to pass us.'

'She could hardly do otherwise, seeing that our table is almost in the middle of the road. Most of the village has been passing and repassing us.'

Götz stiffened, leaning forward, his mouth half open to reveal his uneven, tobacco-stained teeth, his nose twitching like a rabbit's and his albino lashes blinking nervously up and down as he stared at the approaching figure. He looked like some enormous shaggy mongrel, straining at its leash to jump up and pounce.

The girl sauntered forward, eyes lowered in affected indifference, while her companions tittered on each side of her. Then, when she was barely a yard from our table, her glance swept upwards.

Theo crowed with delight, clapping his hands on to his thighs as he rocked backwards and forwards. 'At me! It was at me that she looked!'

'Nonsense,' Götz said crossly. 'She looked at all of us.'

But the extraordinary thing was that, without any doubt, it was at Theo she had looked.

'I told you,' Theo said. 'Didn't I tell you? The Greeks are all gerentophiles. That's been their tradition—look at Socrates! She looked at me—at me, at me!'

'Oh, shut up,' Götz said rudely.

We sat in silence but for the noise of Theo chuckling to himself and Götz rapping one fist impatiently on the table; until once again the girl could be seen approaching. She now had a spray of lilac in one hand which she kept raising to her small, uptilted nose. 'Now let's see,' Götz said grimly.

This time she was on the outside of the trio, and they came so close to our table that her skirt (a nauseating shade of mauve) brushed against the side. Something fell. But such was her deftness that, at first, we had no idea from where it had fallen. Beside Theo's cup there was now a spray of lilac.

'Well?' Theo asked triumphantly. 'What do you make of that?'

'It's no nearer your cup than mine—or Frank's.'

Theo measured the distance with his hand. 'Twice as far to Frank, three times as far to you,' he said. It needed no proof; one could see it with one's eye.

'She couldn't look to see where she was dropping it. She just dropped it. That's all. It was meant for all of us.'

Theo clapped his hands for the waiter, with obvious satisfaction. 'Let's be on our way,' he said.

'Oh, no. Let's stay a moment,' Götz protested. 'Then we can ride back in the cool of the evening.'

'The sun has set,' Theo said. 'And once the sun sets, you will find that in Greece the volta quickly terminates. But as you wish.'

Glumly we sat: I amused myself by listening to the conversation of the three old men seated at the next-door table (it was difficult to make out whether the one who was talking, was talking about his wife or his goat) and Theo began to clean, first his nails with a tooth-pick and then his ears with a corner of his handkerchief. Götz was now not merely rapping with his fists but also stamping his feet in the dust in a disjointed rhythm.

'Please don't do that,' Theo said. 'There's dust enough already.'

The girl did not return.

'I think I shall stretch my legs for a moment, before we go on.' Götz got up and shambled off, hitching at his shorts, while Theo shouted after him:

'I should have thought you could stretch your legs just as well on your bicycle.' He turned to me: 'It's so undignified, this kind of behaviour. Village girls! I have to think of my name; I'm so well known.'

It seemed late for Theo to begin to think of his name; but naturally I did not say so.

Götz returned and sat down moodily. Theo put out a hand and playfully tweaked the albino hairs on one bare thigh:

'Didn't I say that the volta always ends at sunset? Mummy knows best.'

At that moment both Theo and I imagined that this affair, like so many others, had come to its end: we would bicycle away, the girl would discuss us that evening with her friends, and by next week everything would be forgotten. Yet, for once, the established pattern was broken; Götz did not forget.

For days, when there was a silence in our conversation, he would suddenly refer to the girl; he would wonder who she was, what her name might be, whether she went to school or worked, how old she was, where she lived. 'I don't know how you expect me to know the answers to such questions,' Theo would say irritably.

'I don't expect you to know them.'

'Then it seems futile to ask the questions in the first place.'

'I was just wondering.' Götz would sigh, smoothing down his hair with the palm of one hand. 'She was very beautiful.'

When next Sunday came round he inevitably suggested that we should make an excursion to the same beach; but, instead of giving what both Theo and I knew to be the true reason, he mumbled: 'It was so beautiful there— it's quite the best beach in Attica.'

'And quite the worst road,' Theo retorted. 'I, for one, am certainly not going to do that bicycle ride again. If you want to go, you will have to go without me.'

'Please, Theo! You yourself said what fun the day had been.'

'Many things are fun when one does them for the first time,' Theo replied sententiously. 'That does not necessarily mean that they bear repetition. . . . No, my dear. Do by all means visit your—your beach, but don't count on me as your companion.'

Götz hesitated, agonisingly divided between his desire to go back to the village and his loyalty to Theo; Sunday had always been the day they spent together. Then he said with a morose resignation: 'All right, I'll go another time.'

'Please don't alter your plans on my account,' was Theo's somewhat ungracious reply.

But by the following Sunday Götz could deny himself no longer. 'You'll come, won't you, Frank?' he pleaded with me after Theo had persisted in refusing.

I, too, felt as Theo did, that our last visit had been one of those adventures which it becomes tedious to repeat, but when I looked into Götz's face, like that of a child's who is desperately anxious to be given something and yet fearful of being refused, I had to accede. 'Yes, I'll come,' I said.

The stones in the road seemed even larger, the mud thicker, the sun hotter, as we toiled towards our goal. But Götz never stopped singing, as his vast thighs thrust him through the countryside. Once more we bathed; once more we ate our picnic lunch, perched on some rocks; once more we lay back and dozed until the sun was setting. But all these things were done by Götz in a curiously perfunctory manner: they were, after all, no more than a routine that prepared for the evening.

I was afraid that the girl would not be there; but she was, with the same companions, the fat one and the thin one, and in the same skirt of nauseating mauve. When he first saw her, Götz caught his breath in the back of his throat with a rasping, spluttering sound; the colour left his face and then seeped back, crimson. It would have been comic, if it had not been pathetic.

This time we did not sit at the café, but ourselves strolled with the strolling crowds. The first time we passed her the girl did not look; the second time, she glanced up momentarily from under lowered lids; the third time she gave a cold, reproving stare; the fourth time she and her companions all swept past with lowered heads, giggling wildly; the fifth time her eyes flashed with a provocative impudence. It was not until the sixth time that she gave a small, furtive smile.

It seemed to me a meagre return for so much effort; my legs had begun to ache, the back of my throat and my eyes were smarting from the dust. But Götz was overjoyed. 'Did you see that? Did you see that, Frank? She smiled at me—she smiled!'

'Yes, I saw.'

Once again she smiled, and then she disappeared.

From then Götz paid frequent visits to the village and, since he always urged me to accompany him, I too would sometimes go. It seemed to me an extraordinarily laborious wooing: as Götz won now a smile, now a murmured 'Good evening', now a passing comment, and now, at long last, a few words under the shadow of some trees where the volta ended, he appeared to me like a man who, scaling a mountain, slips back two yards for each three he conquers. But to Götz the effort was worthwhile; he was determined to reach the top. Sometimes he was full of elation; at other times he would return in the blackest gloom—she had not been there, she had been talking to some village youth, she had merely nodded instead of smiling. When things had gone badly, it was impossible to cheer him up: he did not wish to go out, to eat or even to do his usual chores around the house.

'Oh, for heaven's sake!' Theo exclaimed on one such occasion. Always so patient in the past towards Götz's infatuations, even a mention of this girl could now exasperate him beyond all endurance: it was as if he sensed that this was different from all those other affairs. 'If you want a woman, George the pastry-cook has an excellent one for you. She's just nineteen, and he tells me that she's in the pink of condition. She's working as a maid at the Abyssinian Legation. She's from Chios—and you know how warm all the Chiotes are!' George the pastry-cook, whom I had never met but of whom I had heard often, was Theo's chief 'agent'—as Theo himself called him. 'George has himself tried her out,' he added.

'Theo—don't, don't, don't!' Götz cried in an agony of protest. He put his clumsy paws to his ears and rocked from side to side. 'How can you make such *degraded* suggestions? I don't want *a* woman. Can't you understand? I only want *one* woman. And you know who that is. It's so vulgar to talk as you were talking. Sometimes I think——'

'All right, all right, there's no need to get hysterical. When you're my age, you'll realise that one woman—or one man, for that matter—is very much like another. If only you could see how foolish and absurd you are being!'

Certainly Götz's situation at that moment had about it all the folly and absurdity which seem to be inseparable from any profound love affair. It was, as Theo had discovered, easy enough to ridicule him and, through that ridicule, to sharpen the agony in which his days were passed. 'Fancy getting yourself into such a state over some common village slut' was the general tenor of his mockery: and because Götz himself was conscious of the humiliation of being pointed out and commented on and even laughed at in the village, he would wince each time that Theo drove this barb home. No lover needs to be told when he is making a fool of himself; he knows already.

Yet surely, I used to say both to myself and sometimes, in consolation, to Götz, Theo himself must, at some stage in his life, have been in the same classic predicament? Surely he, too, had loitered away an evening outside a house, waiting for a face at a window or the sound of an opening door; surely he, too, must have sent notes which he had later regretted, had then waited in agony for a reply, telling himself that the note had fallen into the wrong hands, or had caused annoyance, or had never been delivered at all, and had, at last, decided that all was over. He, too, must have discussed interminably how to interpret a word, a nod, a smile; he, too, must have complained of sleeplessness, an inability to eat, and vague pains and feelings of nausea; he too must have neglected his work, his friends, and all his other interests. Above all he, too, must have known those feelings of exaltation combined with utter abasement.

Yet now he behaved towards Götz as if the German were guilty of the most unusual and shameful kind of conduct.

Typical of this period is one incident which, of many other incidents of a similar nature, clings to my mind. Götz had been told by the girl (whose name, we now discovered, was Kiki) that on a certain evening she would be coming to Patissia to visit an aunt. When she left she would be in the company of an older, married cousin who 'understood', and if Götz would wait for her outside the house between half past ten and eleven, they could walk to the 'bus together. Götz was delighted. From tea-time onwards he did nothing but fidget, making Theo exclaim: 'You really ought to see a doctor—that's the third time you've wee-wee'd in the last hour and a half. . . . Do settle to something! You make me feel so restless.'

When we had supper Götz, who had been left to stir the scrambled eggs, let them burn in the pan: an accident

which he could afford to shrug away as he himself did not
wish to eat anything.

'*Must* we have the radio while we chew on this carbon?'
Theo asked acidly. 'And if we do have it, can we please
stick to one station?'

At a quarter to ten Götz rose to his feet. 'Well . . .'
He pulled his sweater down so that it approximately
joined his trousers; it had shrunk when he had washed it
the day before. 'I suppose I'd better go. Wish me luck!'

'It's only a quarter to ten. You can get to Patissia in
less than a quarter of an hour,' I told him.

'But the 'buses may be full.'

'Not as late as this.'

'Or I may have difficulty in finding the house.'

'You know the number, don't you?'

'Yes.'

I drew back the curtain from the window. 'It's begun
to rain. You don't want to stand needlessly in the rain.'

'I think I ought to go.'

'Just as you like. . . . Shall I come with you?'

'Would you?' His melancholy immediately brightened
into eagerness. 'It'll make waiting so much easier. We
can talk together.'

I knew from experience that conversation with Götz
was impossible at such moments, but I nodded and said:
'All right. I'll come.'

'Unwise, Frank,' Theo said. 'You shouldn't take these
risks with your health.' Ever since my operation Theo
had persisted in regarding me as an invalid whenever it
suited him. 'These autumn evenings are chilly and, if you
get yourself soaked, you may have a nasty bout.' He

seemed even to be jealous of my sympathy for Götz. 'You can be quite sure that she won't turn up anyway.'

We pulled on mackintoshes and borrowed from Theo a vast umbrella, green with age, under which we both ran for the 'bus.

Outside the house in Patissia we waited, huddled together. Götz said: 'When she comes—you won't mind if . . . if . . .'

I smiled: 'I shall leave you both together. You'll find me at that café.' I pointed up the road.

Götz squeezed my shoulder. Then he asked: 'But *will* she come?'

'It's only just half past ten.'

'Yes, that's true.'

Twice he thought he heard the door; once a hand raised the blind but we could see no face. 'Do you think this is the right house?' he inevitably asked.

'I don't know. Haven't you got the number written down?'

He pulled out a cheap note-book and flicked through the pages, holding it up so that it caught the light of a street-lamp. 'Forty-three,' he said. 'That seems to be right.' Then he added: 'But perhaps there are two forty-threes.'

'Oh, that doesn't seem likely.'

'One never knows in Greece.'

I agreed that one never knew.

'Or perhaps there are two Capodistria Streets,' he added. 'What do you think?'

'I have never heard of any one but this.'

'Shall I ask that policeman?'

'If you like.'

'Well, hold the umbrella.'

He returned, shaking his head sadly:

'This is it. And it's past eleven o'clock.' A chill, damp silence followed: I was by now cold enough to believe in Theo's prophecy that I would suffer 'a nasty bout'. I shivered, and stamped my feet.

Götz said: 'Perhaps it was not today.'

'What?'

'Perhaps it was not today. Perhaps it was another day.'

'What date did she say?'

Again the note-book was held to the light. 'October the twenty-seventh. Thursday. . . . What is the date today?'

'October the twenty-seventh.'

'Are you sure?'

'Positive.'

'Thursday?'

'Thursday.'

At twenty minutes to twelve, I said: 'Let's go, Götz. There's no point in waiting. Is there?'

'But she may come yet.'

'She won't be as late as this. She'll have to take a 'bus to Calamos and walk four miles from there. The last 'bus to Calamos leaves at eleven.'

'How do you know that?'

'Because I once took it.'

'There may be a new schedule.'

In the end it was not until ten past twelve that we

eventually moved off. 'What do you think has happened?' Götz asked. 'Do you think she's ill?'

'She may have a cold.'

'Perhaps her mother and father have discovered about us.'

'Would that matter?'

'Oh, yes! She says that they mustn't know—on any account.'

'I don't understand these extraordinary tabus in Greece.'

'Perhaps she's sick of me.'

'Oh, nonsense.'

'Perhaps she just told me to go there to pay me out.'

'Why should she want to pay you out?'

When we reached home, all these possible explanations were once more reviewed before Theo, who was sitting in his dressing-gown at the fire, sipping some cocoa and munching a petit-beurre. His beret was on his head: I often wondered if he slept in it.

'What do you think, Theo?' Götz eventually asked, when Theo had failed to make any contribution to the discussion.

Theo bit decisively into his biscuit, and then examined the bite as he said: 'Frankly, my dear boy, this topic bores me.' He got up and went into his bedroom.

There was a silence in which I was conscious of nothing but Götz's shock and pain. He carefully put another piece of coal on to the fire, the tongs trembling clumsily in his hand, and then he looked at me and asked: 'Tell me, Frank, have I become an awful bore?'

No man should ask that question of another and I was

at a loss how to answer: for the truth was that under all my feelings of friendship and sympathy and pity for Götz there was an ever-increasing ennui. It is, after all, only our own sufferings that manage to hold unending interest for us.

'Have I?' he repeated.

'No, of course not.'

He got up and, clutching the mantelpiece with both hands, began to rock himself backwards and forwards on his heels. 'I know I'm beginning to get on Theo's nerves. I can see that. But what am I to do? I can't help it.' Now he leant forward, his enormous buttocks protruding, and scanned his face in the blotched mirror, stuck with old picture postcards, invitations and newspaper cuttings, that hung over the mantelpiece. 'My God, I am ugly!' he at last broke the silence.

It was a horrible moment and unable to watch him any longer as he stood there, confronting his own reflection, I got up and said: 'Would you like some cocoa? I'm going to make myself some, before I go home.'

'I'll make it.'

'No, you stay here. It'll warm us up,' I added.

As I passed Theo's room, the door was ajar and the candle, which he always said that he preferred to a bedside lamp, was sending shadows flickering over the pink-and-white smoothness of his Victorian washbasin and jug. Theo himself I could not see, since his bed was behind the door.

'Who's that?' he called. 'Götz?'

'No, me.'

'Ah, Frank. Are you going, dear boy?'

177

'Not yet. Can I make some cocoa for Götz and myself?'

'Of course. . . . But come in here first.'

Theo was not in bed, as I had expected, but seated on the edge of it, his bare feet dangling, yellow and crumpled-looking, and his hands in the sleeves of his worn tartan dressing-gown, while he rocked backwards and forwards, making the springs creak. His face, under the beret, looked perplexed and despondent. Lying on the floor was an old copy of *The Illustrated London News* which he had presumably dropped there while he was reading it.

'So Götz's girl didn't turn up?' he said.

'No. I think if I hadn't been there he would have stayed outside the house for the whole night.'

'What kind of madness is this!' he muttered, rocking faster and faster. I did not give an answer; the words did not seem to require one. 'It *is* madness, isn't it?'

'But, Theo, surely you've felt the same, many times. I know that I have.'

'Of course everyone feels the same,' Theo said crossly. 'But we don't all make such a fuss about it. The boy has no self-control whatever.'

'I think he's suffering a lot.'

Theo brooded on this in silence; then he demanded: 'So you think I'm unsympathetic?'

'No—o. Only . . .'

'Well, you do, don't you?' Again he rocked back to a noisy creaking of springs. 'And I am,' he added surprisingly. 'I don't know what's the matter with me. I never used to be like this. Now I just feel I can't stand any more

178

of these emotional messes, like—like so many pieces of raw meat being handed back and forth.' He stared at the candle, the warts on his long, gruyère cheese face throwing monstrous shadows as the flickering light caught them. 'But I must try.' He sighed. 'I must try to understand—to make things easier for him. Poor boy! It's not that I'm not fond of him.'

'No, of course not. He knows that.'

'Does he? Do you think he really does?'

'I'm sure of it.'

Theo got off the bed, and stooped and fumbled under it to draw out a pair of slippers, trodden down at the heels, which were made of the same tartan as his dressing-gown. 'Now you go back to the fire and keep warm, and I'll make your cocoa.'

'No, really, Theo; you'll catch cold in nothing but your dressing-gown.'

'I won't catch cold. I'm tough.' He tightened the dressing-gown cord about his waist and, curiously stiff and erect, made for the door. 'You go and talk to Götz.'

Five minutes later he returned with a tray on which were two mugs of cocoa and a saucer of crumbling petit-beurre biscuits. 'There!' He put the tray down on the top of the piano, and brought a mug first to me and then to Götz where he lay moody and silent, outstretched on the divan.

'Thank you, Theo,' he muttered.

Theo sat down beside him. 'Poor Götz!' he said; as he smiled at the German his face expressed nothing but tenderness and sympathy and affection. Then he looked

179

down at Götz's feet: 'Gracious!' he exclaimed. 'Look how wet you've got yourself. You must take those off at once.' As Götz sipped the hot cocoa, Theo began to unlace his shoes and ease them off to display the soiled socks beneath.

9

I T is from this evening that I date the reinvigoration that started Theo on the third, and last, of the schemes by which he attempted to establish himself as something more durable than a mere 'character' in Athens. Slowly those periods of despondency became shorter, and less and less frequent; he was once more eager to go out, to hear news of his friends and enemies, and himself to plot for their happiness or unhappiness. Perhaps it was simply that he had got used to the idea of life without Nadia; perhaps, as he himself would have explained, he was exchanging a 'manic' for a 'depressive' phase in his life.

'I see now that I've been on the wrong track. Mine is an original genius, and I must do original things. Others have designed clothes, others have been composers. But there is only one fantasiometrist in the world—in the universe. That, when I die, will be the contribution by which I shall be remembered.'

Once again all the old apparatus for publicity and promotion was brought into play. Letters were sent to the newspapers, often bearing the signatures of Theo's friends though he himself composed them; interviews were given to a *Time* magazine reporter, to a poet art-critic, lecturing for the British Council, and to the young editress of a

University magazine; plans were laid for hiring a gallery, borrowing two rooms in the house of a friend, transporting the whole exhibition to Rome, London or Paris, getting Picasso or the Turkish Foreign Minister or Katina Paxinou to open it. But, always recurrent, there remained a single problem: money.

Cecil was due to return, and Theo would sometimes hint that perhaps, once more, he would be willing to give his assistance. 'But I don't like to ask him. It doesn't seem fair. . . . Not that a hundred pounds or so can really matter much to him—can it? I'm told that he's very rich.'

'A hundred pounds always matters—however rich one is,' Götz said sagely.

'And anyway he has the idea now that any project of mine is bound to end in fiasco—simply because, on the two previous occasions, circumstances all conspired against me. . . . Frank, can't you think of a patron for me? Wouldn't the British Council do something?'

'But, Theo, fantasiometry has so very little to do with the British Way of Life.'

'Oh, that attitude is so parochial!'

I shrugged my shoulders.

'What about your friend, Madame Landerlöst?' I was astonished that Theo should mention her, since he had always insisted on placing on her shoulders the blame for his failure with Mabel Aaronson.

'What about her?'

'Their Embassy is one of the largest in Athens.'

'But why should she——?'

'She's interested in art, isn't she?'

'Up to a point.'

'And in Greece?'

'Well—yes.'

'Then there you are!'

At the time I did not take this suggestion any more seriously than the others that Theo had been throwing out during the last few days. But two mornings later, he was round early at Dino's flat, coming into my bedroom while I was dressing, with a cardboard box under his arm. 'I was afraid you'd be off for a lesson before I could get to you. Really, Dino should speak to that man of his —his manners are awful. I had to push past him, he didn't want me to come in!' He watched me for a moment as I brushed my hair before the glass, and then said, with obvious pleasure: 'Goodness, you *are* going thin in front. Still—you're the sort of person who looks far more distinguished when he's bald.' He put the box down on my unmade bed, and seating himself beside it, began to tug at the string. 'I had a brain-wave,' he said. He chuckled to himself: 'There's not much I don't know about diplomacy.' Continuing to struggle with the knot he added: 'After this, I think we shall have Madame Landerlöst in the bag.' He glanced up at me, as I began to thread my cuff-links. 'Don't you ever use those shell cuff-links I made you for Christmas?'

'Not for everyday.'

'Look!' He opened the box. 'Sophie Landerlöst!'

I peered in; and the extraordinary thing was that Theo's construction was recognisably Sophie.

'The face is built up from Swedish matches,' he began to explain. 'The eyes are two studs from a pair of climbing

183

boots, and the mouth is painted with some cyclamen lip-stick—I noticed that that was the shade she used. One breast has a photograph of Josephine Baker pasted on it, and the other of Sarah Bernhardt; that suggests her equivocal origins, you see. The breasts themselves are made from two tennis balls from a set of six that I bought many years ago in Paris. In Paris, you notice—most appropriate. At her feet are lying these typical Greek figures, cut from magazines and newspapers, of course: an evzone, Mr Venizelos—always so susceptible—the actor Pappas, Admiral Lappas, a man who has just passed his one hundred and twentieth birthday in Joannina, Mr Yost, the chef at the Grande Bretagne, and so on. . . . That, of course, means that all Greece is at her feet.' He continued to explain, pointing to each feature in turn, until he concluded: 'And now, dear boy, the rest is up to you.'

I drew back, astonished.

'You must take this little gift and present it to Madame Landerlöst.'

'Present it to Madame Landerlöst?' I echoed.

'Well, what's so strange in that? You're having drinks with her today, aren't you?'

'Yes.'

'Good. Then all you have to do is to hand her the box with some—some judiciously worded compliment.'

'But what shall I say? She may be offended.'

'Why should she be offended? She should be honoured that I have singled her out to become a subject for my art.'

'She may not see it like that.'

'Of course she will—if you say the right things.

Naturally that depends on you. But I can rely on you, can't I?'

I hesitated; I knew that this was one of the 'tests' to which, from time to time, Theo would put his friends, and I realised that if I should refuse, there was a likelihood that I should be banished, either temporarily or permanently, from his circle. 'When the hour of need came, he failed me': how often I had heard that sentence applied indiscriminately to friends who had put off his visits, had failed to win for him some concession from the banks or Government offices in which they worked, or all unconsciously had perpetrated some other imagined slight or insult, like forgetting his birthday, failing to recognise him in a crowded street or laughing at some remark that was intended to be serious.

'All right,' I said. 'I'll give it for you. But don't hold me responsible for the consequences.'

'Now is that likely?' Theo asked.

It was, I knew, very likely.

Sophie Landerlöst had told me to 'drop in for a drink —just ourselves, that's all'; but as I had feared, her drawing-room was crowded. I walked towards her with extreme self-consciousness, holding Theo's box. Everyone seemed to be staring at me, and when Sophie herself greeted me, I dithered, not sure what to do with my burden as she held her hand out to be shaken. Eventually, as there was no table, I put the box on the floor. Theo would not have approved, I knew, of the clumsiness of my entry: I might almost have been Götz.

Sophie had a daughter, a girl of nine who, when she was not helping at Sophie's parties, seemed to spend her time sticking photographs of film-stars into an album. She spoke French, English and Greek indiscriminately, often all three at once, and took what I considered to be an unpleasantly precocious interest in all her mother's affairs. Sophie always declared that she had brought her up to be 'an old-fashioned child'; but apart from her habit of curtseying to adults to whom she was introduced and the pert mock-gravity of her manner, her upbringing seemed, on the contrary, to have been disastrously 'modern'. She had a thin, razor-sharp face around which her dark hair fell in elaborate ringlets.

As I stood exchanging a few words with Sophie, this child tiptoed towards us, gave me her usual bobbing curtsey, and then, with the pointed toe of one of the black patent-leather dancing slippers, began surreptitiously to ease the lid off Theo's box.

'Désirée dear! What are you doing? Leave Mr Cauldwell's parcel alone.'

'What's inside it, Mr Cauldwell—please?' Her skinny arms were locked behind her back as she swayed from side to side.

'It's for your mother,' I said. 'Be a good girl and put it on that table for me.'

Sophie had been distracted by another guest, but the child now called out: 'Mummy! Mummy! Mr Cauldwell has a present for you.'

'A present—for me?'

'It's in his box. . . . Can I open it for Mummy, Mr Cauldwell?'

People had begun to gather round. 'It's not from me,' I said. 'It's from a friend of mine—Colonel Grecos.'

Désirée began to giggle: 'Do you mean that old man that I saw putting some of our cigarettes in his pocket when we gave that party for Eisenhower?'

'No, that was Colonel Garvas,' Sophie corrected her. 'Colonel Grecos is that extraordinary old thing who banged out those Greek dances for us that evening—isn't he, Mr Cauldwell?'

I wondered how Theo would feel if he heard his performance of the Athens Concerto described in these terms, but I nodded and said: 'Yes, you came to his house.'

'It was great fun,' Sophie said. She turned to the guests gathered around us: 'We did all the dances—and this old boy is really a wonderful dancer, much better than I. We went on till two.'

'I heard about it from Lady Aaronson,' Mrs Tullett, the wife of a British businessman, said with a certain tartness. 'I gather that you really let yourself go, Sophie.' Although she and her hostess were perpetually in each other's houses, they rarely had a good word to say of each other. 'Lady Aaronson told me you were stinking.'

'I was!'

'Do open the parcel, Mummy. Or may I open it?' Désirée, already kneeling on the floor, began to lift the lid.

'What is it? What on earth is it?' the guests all asked. Everyone turned to me: 'What is it, Mr Cauldwell?'

'Colonel Grecos calls it "fantasiometry".'

'Calls it what? What was that? What?' different voices queried.

Mrs Tullett, who was tall and raw-boned and perpetually conscious of being less wealthy, less well-dressed

187

and less popular than her hostess, drawled: 'It's this thing he does. Somebody—who was it?—was talking about it to me only the other day. It was Madame Tsaldaris, I think —or was it Tiggy Ghika. People seem to think he's got something new.'

'But what is it? What is it meant to be?'

'Guess,' I said.

'It's Mummy!' Désirée cried.

'Right, first time.'

'It's *me*!' Sophie exclaimed with a mingling of incredulity and delight. 'But explain it to me—I don't understand. How clever of the child to realise!' She put an arm round Désirée and pressed her to one of her massive thighs. 'Do explain, Mr Cauldwell.'

I had never thought of myself in the past as being a good salesman, but now it was too easy. I talked vaguely, using the terms that Theo himself would have used, about fantasiometry, and when any statement appeared to be questioned, I had only to wait for Mrs Tullett to silence the interrupter by putting in some remark like: 'But that's obvious' or 'You're missing the whole point of modern art', followed by an inaccurate repetition or expansion of what I had just said.

'But I think it's such fun!' Sophie cried when I had concluded my explanation. 'Don't you? Don't you think it's fun?' She turned to her guests, and then once again, fascinated, examined the object. She turned it this way and that, touched the two tennis-ball breasts with the long crimson nail of her forefinger, and then held it up to her nose to give it a sniff. 'It even smells of me!' she cried.

'I must get him to do one of me,' the wife of a minor Greek politician said.

'So must I,' another woman added.

Mrs Tullett turned to me and said in a hoarse whisper: 'Stupid hens! They'll do anything if they think it's the fashion. As soon as I'd bought my Tsarouchis, there were rude pictures of nude sailors in every flat in Kolonaki. It must be so discouraging for an artist like—like Colonel What's-his-name to have to stomach that sort of enthusiasm.'

But Theo had a stomach for enthusiasm of any sort, and he was delighted to be taken up by these foolish, excitable women who could pay no higher compliment to his art than to say it was 'such fun'. Now he was to be seen at innumerable cocktail parties and tea parties and when there was a knock at the door it was as likely to be two shrill, well-dressed Kolonaki 'hens' (as Mrs Tullett had called them), as two Peiraeus cocks for Cecil. Mrs Tullett herself and Sophie were vying with each other for the honour of being Theo's patroness.

'I don't know what to say. Of course Madame Landerlöst is much *grander*, isn't she? And if I have the exhibition at the Embassy, it'll give it a certain stamp. But Mrs Tullett is much more of an intellectual—people take her much more seriously—and though her house hasn't really got a single good room, if she's willing to let me have both the drawing-room and the dining-room . . . What do you think, Frank?'

'I don't know.'

'That's helpful, anyway. . . . I suppose you haven't got any British Embassy writing paper?'

'No. Why should I?'

Theo was at that moment at work on one of his 'objects'. 'I'm doing Moore Crossthwaite. Next time you're at the Embassy, do see if you can scrounge some. One of those clerks you know is sure to let you have a sheet. But it *must be stiff.*'

In the end, Theo decided that it would be best to hold his exhibition under Sophie's patronage; and inevitably, when this was known, Mrs Tullett, previously so lofty in her championing of his art, now began to scatter derisive comments. 'Oh, it's amusing in a *dotty* sort of way,' one would hear her drawl at parties. 'Not at all a bad joke. But poor Sophie will take such things seriously. She's like a child in many ways . . . Oh, Sophie, we're just talking about your dirty old man. You're not seriously going to organise his exhibition for him, are you?'

'Certainly I am.'

'I think it's so brave of you. Athenians have such a sharp sense of the ridiculous. Anyway, this *is* the silly season so, I suppose, why not?'

As the day they had fixed drew closer and closer, Theo seemed to eat and sleep less and less and work more and more. He became, as a result, nervy and irritable and his tendency to see insults where none were intended had now been aggravated into what can only be described as a definite persecution mania. From time to time even his closest friends—Götz or Cecil or myself—would fall under suspicion, and if two of us ever began to talk together, in front of Theo but out of his hearing, he would shout: 'What are you whispering about? What is it? Out with it!'

The smallest mishap would start him on a train of ominous brooding. For example:

'I wonder if I can really trust Dino?' he mused one evening as he splashed paint on to one of his 'objects'.

'Why not?' I asked.

'Well, it's two days since I gave him that announcement for the editor of *Kathimerini* and it still hasn't appeared. They were going to have dinner together.'

'Do you think Dino forgot it?'

'No, I don't think he *forgot* it.'

'Well, then?'

'There's something not quite straight about him.' He stared at his work, and then looked up at me: 'He might have destroyed the announcement,' he said.

'But, Theo—why on earth?'

The next morning the announcement was on the front page of the newspaper.

Götz and I both realised that the sleeplessness, and the refusal to settle to a proper meal, and the unrelieved tension in which Theo was now living were bound, in the end, to have an adverse effect on his health. We used to urge him to rest, but having lain down on a couch for a few minutes, he would throw off the rug with which he had covered himself, and drag himself to his feet, mumbling, ' "Nox ruit, Aenea . . ." '

'But, Theo, do please sleep for just half an hour.'

'I haven't time.' He would begin pulling odds and ends from a drawer. 'Besides, with all these ideas whirling about inside me, how can I sleep? I must get them out. Must, must, must,' he would go on mumbling as he settled again to work.

Only on one occasion, when Götz had his birthday, did we succeed in dragging him out: and that was the night of the disaster.

Theo was in an excellent mood, for his exhibits, with one or two exceptions, were now all ready, stacked upon shelf upon shelf of the room which he had always called the 'library', although the books had long since been sold during one of his financial crises and the shelves until this moment had supported nothing but dust and some tattered copies of *Punch* and *The Illustrated London News* and *Health and Efficiency*. We had been together to see Sophie Landerlöst about the final arrangements for the exhibition which was to be held in less than ten days.

I was afraid that the lofty self-importance with which Theo now behaved towards both her, her servants and myself might cause her annoyance, but obviously it amused her.

'Yes, I think this room should do,' Theo announced, examining the banquet-hall. 'What a pity about that fire-place—it looks so terribly *nouveau-riche*, doesn't it? . . . But, at any rate, we can have those curtains removed. Perhaps we could have those brocade ones from the dining-room put in their place? The windows seem to be the same size.' He glanced down: 'Of course the floor will need a polish.' Turning to the man-servant, he repeated: 'I said that the floor will need a polish.'

'Of course, sir.'

'And the tables on which we shall put the exhibits.'

'Naturally, sir.'

Sophie winked at me and smiled; and the man-servant, who had been riled by these directions, saw her do so and at once himself began to twitch slightly at the lips as he caught the infection of his mistress's amusement.

'Anything else, Colonel?' Sophie asked.

'May I just once again run an eye over the list of the guests?'

'Certainly.' She gave me a violent nudge. 'What do you feel about Mr Markezinis—ought I to ask him?'

Theo pondered judiciously; but it was obvious that the thought of this guest filled him with excitement. 'H'm—yes,' he said. 'I don't approve of his politics at all. But since this is a gathering of all the Athens intellectuals, well, certainly, I suppose he should be asked. You'd better send the invitation by hand,' he added. 'Posts in Athens are so slow.'

When we reached home, he was so gleeful that he caught Götz in his arms and began to waltz round the room with him. 'And Markezinis is coming—think of that! Think of that, Götz!'

But Götz was in no mood to share his excitement. As soon as he could extricate himself, he slumped on to the couch where he began to gnaw at his fingers: recently he had taken to chewing, not only his nails, but also his knuckles.

'What's the matter, Götz?' I asked.

'This is a fine sort of birthday. She said she'd ring up this evening and she didn't. She said she'd be in the Zappeion at four, and she wasn't. I waited there till six.'

'Poor old thing,' Theo said vaguely. But he was too absorbed in his own happiness to take much notice of Götz's misery. 'If only you'd met that girl that George the pastry-cook——'

193

'Shut up, Theo! Shut up!'

'All right, my dear, all right. There's no need to fly off the handle.'

Cecil appeared in the doorway to his room, rubbing some cream into his hands and easing back his cuticles as he did so. 'I don't know what's the matter with my hands,' he said. 'Feel how rough they are.' He brushed the back of one up my cheek. 'I suppose it's these winds.' He glanced down to where Götz sat slumped, still moodily biting his fingers. 'You don't look awfully gay, ducky. What's up?'

Götz said nothing.

'I've got something here for the birthday-boy.' Cecil drew out of his dressing-gown pocket a packet wrapped in tissue paper, and pressed it into the paw on which Götz was at that moment not engaged. 'With Auntie's fondest love,' he said, kissing Götz on the top of his head.

Götz looked pleased, embarrassed and humiliated, all at the same time, when he unwrapped a new silver cigarette-case. 'Thank you,' he muttered clumsily. 'Thank you, Cecil . . . But really . . .' He weighed it in one hand. 'It's so heavy.'

'Don't let anyone steal it off you. I've had at least a dozen stolen in my life.'

I suggested that we should go out and celebrate Götz's birthday at one of the Peiraeus tavernas; it was a long time since we had made such an expedition, all of us together.

'Good idea!' Theo said, jumping to his feet. 'George the pastry-cook says that there's one near the Turkish harbour where one can smoke *hashish* in the back room. Or we

could go to that other place with the Lesbian singer—
you know, the one with the voice of tungsten steel.
You'll come, won't you, Cecil?'

'Not tonight, I'm afraid. I'm receiving.'

'But surely that can be put off.'

'Wet or fine, rain or shine, goose-girl makes it a
principle never to put anyone off. I haven't many
principles, but that's one of them.'

'Well, join us later.'

'If I'm not utterly whacked.'

We started the evening with tremendous hilarity. Theo
had begun to complain of a headache and Götz was still
brooding morosely when we climbed into a taxi: but
by the time we reached Peiraeus they were both singing
a popular Greek song at the tops of their voices. It was
Saturday night and the taverna was full. Friends we had
made on other occasions when we had come here, began
to shout at us: 'Johnny, come here! . . . Hey, Fritz! . . .
Yassas, boys! . . . Hey, boys! . . . Hey!'

'Do they mean to include me in that "boys" of theirs?'
Theo asked, delighted. He sank into a chair which was
held out to him by a small, grubby sailor whose two
front teeth were missing, and putting his legs up on to
another chair, sighed as he said: 'Well, it's good to be
back. I feel as if I'd just been released from prison. You
know, Frank, it must be nearly a month since we last did
this.' He clicked his fingers above his head, and then
banged on a glass with a fork which he took, without
permission, from the sailor's plate of fried spleen and
lung. The waiter came over, and Theo ordered wine for
us, for this table, for that table, even for the orchestra.

'You're being very extravagant.'

'We must celebrate. Besides, after Monday week, orders will be rolling in. I shall be rich, Frank—you wait and see. Next summer I shall go to England. I shall have an exhibition there—perhaps at your Tate Gallery. Your Tate Gallery is one of the best, isn't it?' He swallowed a glass of retsina at a single gulp. Then he began to giggle: 'But I shall *not* go to the Frinton Festival—definitely not.'

Some sailors and dock-workers to whom Theo had sent one of the cans of wine now raised their glasses and drank to our healths. Theo bowed with tremendous decorum, murmuring to me: 'Amusing boys—the salt of the earth.' One of them called out:

'When will you dance, Theo?'

'When I am drunk.'

Götz said: 'If my Kiki were here!'

'T't, t't!' Theo reproved him. 'Now forget about her! Enjoy yourself and stop that silly brooding!' He raised his glass: 'To our birthday-boy.'

Götz grinned and, shaking himself like a dog, seemed to shake off the melancholy cloud which had, for that moment, once more enveloped him.

Theo, clicking his fingers in time to the music, said: 'This boy *can* dance. Isn't he adorable, Frank?'

It was not the adjective which I myself would have chosen to describe a blue-chinned dock-worker of over six foot, even though he did wear a rose over one ear, but I agreed that he could dance. 'Such control, such rhythm!' Theo exclaimed ecstatically. 'Marvellous.' He picked up the sailor's fork again and harpooning a rubbery square of lung held it up to my mouth. I shook my head and he gave it to Götz.

'It tastes like a bit of tennis ball,' Götz said, swallowing hard. 'Horrible.'

'Just prejudice,' Theo said. 'Just Nordic prejudice.'

At last he decided to dance; and as he stalked out into the small space in front of the orchestra, everyone began to whistle and clap and shout 'Bravo' until, by solemnly raising both hands, he managed to obtain silence. There was a titter as he took off his coat and plucked his beret from his head to hand them to the waiter, and another titter when he took a glass from the brawny fist of the dock-worker whom he had described as 'adorable' and sipped some retsina from it. But no one tittered as soon as he began to dance: for those men knew that, in spite of his age, he could dance better than any of them. Through the coiling cigarette smoke their eyes watched him, intent and admiring.

'How young he looks when he dances!' Götz whispered to me. 'It's incredible.'

During these last weeks of unremitting work Theo had seemed to age; his walk had become slower and stiffer, his right arm would tremble, and the rigidity with which he held himself upright seemed quite as much a mark of old age as if he had stooped. Yet, now, he was dancing with all the fluidity and grace and vigour of the six-foot dock-worker who had been on the floor before him.

'Vonderful!' Götz exclaimed. 'Fantastic!'

Theo was whirling round and round, both arms extended as if they were the magnificent wings of an eagle when, suddenly, he faltered and swayed. His eyes,

197

no longer half closed in that trance which dancing seemed invariably to induce in him, now gave the appearance of searching the room, with growing panic, for something they could nowhere find. Götz pushed back his chair, making an unpleasant grating noise on the stone floor: he, alone, realised at that moment that something was amiss.

Theo swayed again and the two raised arms were extended as though to grapple with some invisible object. Then he fell: not violently, but folding up, first the legs, then the torso, and finally the neck and head. There were some titters from those who thought he had merely tripped; others looked at each other, first questioning and then in alarm. Götz rushed over and I rushed after him. But Theo was already struggling to get up.

'What happened?' he asked in a strangely dreamy voice. 'Where am I? I can't remember . . .' We helped him back to his chair, at the same time trying to keep away the crowds that were gathering round. Theo sat down, crossed his arms over the table, and rested his head on his arms. He shook his head from side to side, and stamped with his right foot repeatedly on the floor, as though it had pins and needles.

'What's the matter?' someone asked. 'Is he ill?' came from another.

'Nothing, nothing,' Götz said. 'He's feeling faint, that's all. Please go back to your places.'

Slowly they drifted back, glancing over their shoulders at us and muttering to each other.

Theo raised his head: 'I can't see properly,' he said. 'What happened? What was I doing?'

'You'll be all right,' Götz assured him. 'I'll go out and find a taxi. You stay here with him, Frank. We'd better get him home.'

'But I don't want to go home,' Theo said obstinately. 'I'm quite all right now. It was just for a moment—I felt so odd. It must have been the heat.' He caught Götz's sleeve as the German rose: 'Don't let's go yet!'

'I think we'd better, Theo. You ought to get to bed.'

'But I'm all right—really I am!'

However in the end we persuaded him to do as we wanted.

By the time we had helped him into the taxi, he had completely recovered. 'Silly of me to do a thing like that,' he said. 'I suppose I must have frightened you both. Apart from spoiling poor Götz's birthday party. I'm sorry, my dear.' He squeezed Götz's hand. 'We must go out again another evening. Do please forgive me. Next time I won't dance. I'm afraid the truth is that I'm too old for dancing now.'

He refused to allow us to assist him up the stairs of his house and, though the key trembled in his hand so that he had difficulty in getting it into the lock, he insisted on opening the door himself.

As we stepped into the hall and I groped for the light switch, Cecil's voice called: 'Who's that? What is it?' He was in his bedroom.

'It's only us,' I shouted, surprised by his nervousness.

'Oh, thank God! . . . Come here, Frank.'

I went into the bedroom, and found Cecil curled up into a ball at the foot of the bed with the blankets and sheets pulled haphazard round him to cover everything but part of his bald head, his eyes and his nose. 'What's the matter?' I asked.

Cecil began to sob in a curiously long, gulping spasm; it was horrible.

'Cecil, what is it?'

He raised his pear-shaped face a little from the cocoon of bedclothes and I saw that a red patch stretched across one of his cheeks from nostril to ear. He hiccoughed: 'I can't tell you what I've been through. I can't tell you. Even the thought of it makes me feel ghastly. Please don't ask me! I can't tell you!'

Götz and Theo had now joined us, looking in amazement at Cecil.

Eventually Theo said: 'Well, never mind. Now you've learned your lesson. No great harm has been done. Götz can dress that bruise of yours. . . . Have you—er—lost anything?'

'Oh, only sixty drachmae. . . . It's not—not *that*!'

'Well, then what are you crying about? Come—be a man!' I felt that Theo's efforts at consolation, however well-intentioned, were nevertheless clumsy. 'Come along. You can't lie there—it's too early for bed. Come and have a drink with us.'

'But, Theo . . . It's . . . it's . . . your exhibition!' Cecil at last got out.

'*What!*' Theo exclaimed.

Theo flung open the study door: 'My God!' we heard him exclaim. He went in.

Götz and I followed. The whole carpet, usually a faded maroon, was now white with powdered glass, plaster of Paris and a confetti-like litter of paper. My eye caught an extraordinary assortment of objects: one of Sophie's tennis-ball breasts, a screwed-up sheet of Embassy paper, a hat-pin that had belonged to the Baroness Schütz, a French sailor's cap, the pom-pom from an evzone's shoe, a jagged piece of glass that had been part of Nadia's bottle of bath-salts . . . I had seen nothing like this since the air-raids in London.

Theo was on his knees in the midst of the rubble. He picked up these objects, one after another; sometimes he would hold two pieces together; sometimes he would slip one into his pocket or put it back on the shelves. Then, slowly, the realisation came to him that the damage was beyond repair. Either he must begin again or he must forget his whole art.

Slowly he rose to his feet: he was trembling and white, and yet, at that moment, he had a dignity far greater than any he had possessed before.

'So that's that,' he said.

He gave a small, slightly crooked smile at Götz and myself as he limped towards his bedroom.

'HOW nice of you, Frank my dear, to leave Dino's bunfight early to bring me your Christmas wishes.' Three months ago I would have suspected a sarcasm in the words, for once again Dino had omitted to send either Theo or Götz an invitation to a party; but since 'the calamity' (as Theo himself would refer to it) there had been a remarkable softening and weakening in the old man's nature. I had expected him to be wholly crushed, and then bitterly resentful: but he had accepted this final defeat with a serenity and resignation that did him the greatest credit. Even Cecil had never been reproached, and apart from now always speaking of him as 'that sissy', Theo had, to my knowledge, said no word against him.

'Götz and I were singing some of the old carols together.' Theo was at the piano. 'They give one a feeling of pleasant melancholy, don't they? Every Christmas Eve, when we were children, we used to gather round the piano and sing them with my mother. Oh, how long ago it seems!' He sighed: 'How long, long ago!' Then he shook himself: 'But I mustn't be sentimental—I know you don't like it. Have some whisky; don't be afraid, it's real Scotch whisky. Cecil sent it from Italy by a sailor friend. Wasn't that kind of him? Help yourself!'

I poured myself a glass and, raising it, said: 'Happy Christmas!'

'Happy Christmas to you, dear boy!' Theo hoisted himself slowly from the piano stool, straightened his beret and tightened the knot of his dressing-gown, before he held out a Christmas card: 'Pretty, isn't it? From Daphne Bath. . . . This is from Maurice Bowra.' He held out another. 'This is from William Faulkner. As you know, I don't read novels—not even yours—but they tell me that he's good. We climbed Olympus together.' Proudly he showed me one after another of the cards, taking them from the mantelpiece, with the conclusion: 'Yes, I have a lot of good friends. I've never wanted for friends.'

'Have you seen the Christmas tree that the Swedes have sent?' Götz asked. 'Theo and I thought of going out to look at it.'

'*I* thought of going out to look at it,' Theo corrected with a twinkle. 'Götz thought of going out to meet Kiki. Didn't you, Götz?'

Götz looked down at the carpet, grinned and blushed.

'She's supposed to be spending Christmas Eve with her cousin, and her cousin seems to be a modern and sensible woman. Kiki thinks she can get away after midnight,' Theo explained.

'Let's go,' Götz said. He was obviously nervous and impatient to be off.

Although it was only a few minutes before midnight the streets were deserted. As we walked, we would hear from the houses that we passed the sounds of dance music, laughter and shouting. Theo had linked an arm in either of ours; he strode out between us, vigorous and exultant. 'So many Christmases,' he reminisced. 'And I think the happiest I ever spent was with your British boys in hospital in Salonica. That was in nineteen-sixteen. I was recovering from typhoid, and you wouldn't expect a Christmas to be happy under such circumstances, would you? I shall never forget the fun we had. There was a sister—Sister Agnes, I think—and a doctor who came from a place called West—or was it East?—Kirby . . .' Happily he ran on: they had played a practical joke on one of the other patients—a greedy sergeant-major—by pretending to forget to serve him; and when they had at last served him, the doctor had snatched the plate away, saying that the food would be bad for him. . . . Theo chuckled to himself. 'What a sense of humour! What a priceless sense of humour! Only the English can play jokes like that!'

A few people, singly or in couples, were wandering round the vast, glittering Christmas tree: they looked bemused and child-like, the coloured lights reflected in their pale, upturned faces. Theo wandered with them, exclaiming: 'Ah, beautiful, beautiful!'

Götz glanced everywhere: 'I can't see her,' he said.

'It's not yet twelve,' I encouraged him. 'Don't be impatient.'

'I do hope she'll come.'

Theo returned to us with a bag of chestnuts in one hand. 'Look what I've found! . . . Eat!' He held out the bag.

Götz shook his head: 'I don't feel hungry.'

Suddenly Kiki had run out from the shadows. In front of all of us, she was, not unnaturally, embarrassed and shy;

but when she and Götz wandered off alone together, to examine the tree, they had their arms twined about each other. Theo ate another chestnut: 'I do hope it'll all come out all right in the end,' he said. 'But from a worldly point of view, Götz has so little to offer.'

When midnight struck, Theo clapped his hands: 'Come, we must sing Auld Lang Syne! Götz—Kiki! Come here!' Peremptorily he gathered together all the drifting couples, and making us link hands round the tree, he led us off with the first bars:

> 'Should old acquaintance be forgot
> And never brought to mind . . .'

Slowly we began to circle, Theo's cracked, yet vigorous, baritone floating up into the clear sky until one by one we had all joined in.

At the end Götz whispered to us: 'Kiki says she can come. Is that all right, Theo?'

'All right? Of course!'

We got into a taxi, Theo sitting in front and the rest of us behind, and I passed the journey staring out of my window while Götz and Kiki surreptitiously pecked at each other and whispered endearments. When we reached home, Theo pushed Götz and Kiki into the sitting-room, with what seemed to me to be an unbecoming haste, and then shut the door. 'Come with me to the kitchen, Frank. I don't suppose they'll stay long *there*,' he added. 'I'm so glad for dear Götz's sake. And after all she's not a bad-looking little slut.'

'She's not a slut, Theo. And she's really most attractive.'

I had seldom seen Theo more sprightly and gleeful.

He tiptoed, beckoning me after him, down the passage that led to his kitchen and then stamped out wildly at the cockroaches which scuttled away across the stone floor as he turned on the light. Everywhere dirty crockery and cutlery was piled in heaps, and a lean cat was wriggling between mountains of plates which it threatened, at any moment, to send crashing from the table.

'Pssst!' Theo hissed and the cat bounced to the floor. 'It's not always like this. But my old girl is away for Christmas, and Götz has been so distracted these last few days that he has quite neglected the house.'

He picked up a fork and went over to the vast iron range on which a saucepan was spluttering and sizzling.

'What are you cooking?' I asked.

'It's my surprise. Götz knows nothing about it.'

He took off the lid of the saucepan which was so hot that he dropped it to the floor with a curse and a loud clatter, and then began to fish inside with the fork. Finally he raised a khaki-coloured object.

'There!' he said. 'I made it myself.'

'But what is it?'

'A Christmas pudding of course. It's going to be excellent. It may not *look* very professional,' he added, 'but that's because I had to wrap it up in one of my hand-kerchiefs. I can promise you that it'll taste good. Just unwrap it for me, there's a good boy, and I'll go and warn Götz that we shall be interrupting him for five minutes.'

'Wouldn't he rather be left alone?'

'He's got the whole night,' Theo said sharply.

When he returned he was giggling joyfully: 'Would

you believe it? **Quick work!** They're already in bed.'
He took down a **bottle** of brandy from a shelf on which
there also rested a **pair** of old shoes, the broken half of a
plate, a mug from the Coronation of George VI, and
three soiled stiff collars. 'Well, I'm very glad for Götz's
sake,' he repeated. '**That** boy needs a break.' Liberally, he
began to splash the cognac over the pudding. Then he
ran out into the hall and broke a sprig of holly off the
dusty branch which hung from the electric light.

'I only hope I can find some clean plates. . . . Ah well,
we shall have to use these saucers. Now get the bottle of
champagne out of the ice-box. . . . No, that's not the ice-
box—that's the coal-box. The other one! Good boy!'

Gradually everything was assembled on the tray.

'Now you go ahead of me and open the door. They're
in Götz's room. But first put a light to the pudding.'

Götz and Kiki lay, with an extraordinary smiling
unself-consciousness, side by side on the high iron bed-
stead. The room was in darkness, as Theo and I entered,
and we could see each other only by the blue-green
flames that lapped round the pudding. Theo was singing:
'God rest you merry, gentlemen . . .' as he marched in
ceremoniously and placed the tray on the foot of the bed.
Kiki had drawn the sheet up over one shoulder, but the
other was bare and glimmered in the reflection of the
flames at which we were all staring. Her black hair was
loose and fell all about her.

'Put on the lamp,' Theo said to me, as the flames began
to die, 'but cover it with this scarf of mine.' He unknotted
his scarf.

'So, a Happy **Christmas**, children!' Solemnly he went

to the bed and kissed first Kiki and then Götz on the forehead. He came to me: 'Will you be outraged if I kiss you too?'

'No, of course not.'

He kissed me. 'I don't know why, I feel extraordinarily happy.'

'So do we all,' I said.

IT was some consolation that Theo died with so little pain and fuss: between the stroke that, on New Year's Day, deprived him of the use of his right arm and the second stroke that killed him, less than a week passed. Curiously, even after the first mild stroke, he seemed to guess he would not recover.

We had wanted to send him to a hospital, but he had protested: 'No, no, let me stay here! If I'm going to die, it must be in my own bed. And you and Götz look after me so well. I should hate to be pawed about by a lot of strange women. But perhaps I'm being an awful nuisance to you both?' he asked with the pathetic consideration which from the first moment of his illness he had never ceased to show us. 'Am I?'

'No, of course not, Theo,' we both protested.

Götz, having trained in a hospital, took on himself most of the actual nursing and it was left to me either to sit with Theo and read to him or to go out on errands for medicine and food. Theo's choice of book was curious: that Victorian classic *Misunderstood*. I, myself, found it nauseating in its sentimentality, but Theo would sigh and exclaim: 'Beautiful . . . beautiful . . . beautiful . . . Oh, Frank, if you knew how I wept over those pages when I was thirteen! How I wept!' And even now the tears would form in the corners of his eyes.

When I was not reading, he would wish to talk: sometimes about his childhood, sometimes about his exploits in the Air Force, sometimes about Nadia, but most often about poor Götz. What was to become of him? he would ask me. If only he had something to leave the boy! Of course he would get the house and all that was in it, but how would he keep it up? 'I have no money to leave him. . . . Oh, how terrible it is to think of the thousands that I squandered! Terrible!' And he would shift restlessly from side to side, dragging the bedclothes with him.

Perhaps Götz could turn the house into a private hotel, Theo suggested one morning: it was obvious that he had been occupied with this idea for most of a sleepless night, for he now began to go into the most minute of details—what rent he should charge; the sort of clients he should aim to attract ('nothing smart, of course, but nothing Bohemian'); the alterations that would have to be made. 'But, Theo, do please stop worrying about all this until you are well. Götz will be all right.'

'I never wanted to leave him high and dry. But what can I do? My pension stops with me.' On and on he would pursue the same subject until I suggested that I should begin to read again.

He seemed to be curiously indifferent to dying; he even talked about it with a melancholy resignation: 'I've no real regrets at going,' he murmured with that thickening of his speech that I had found the most upsetting feature of his stroke. 'I shall be sorry not to see my friends, and I should like to have gone back to Corfu once more. Yes,

I would like to have seen Pelakas—my village—for another spring. Well, *dis aliter visum*.' He sighed. 'I used to fear death so much; even up to six months ago. And now—I couldn't care less, to use that vulgar modern English phrase.' He smiled: 'I think I can say I've been happy; yes, I think I can say that. It only needs courage—and faith. Faith, above all. You remember the firewalking—the firewalking, Frank?' I nodded and said yes. 'Well, for someone like myself—someone so *different*—life is like that firewalking. If one has absolute faith in one's own rightness and the wrongness of the world—as those firewalkers do—then one can get across without being burned. But if one lacks that absolute faith then, like poor Götz that day at Langada, one suffers—one suffers so much! . . . Well, thank God, I've had that faith: I've managed to get across with no more than a minor blister or two.'

After I had read to him the penultimate chapter of *Misunderstood*, he again began to talk. He was mumbling and I had to stoop down to hear what he was saying. 'I should like to be remembered for *something*,' he was saying. 'For my dress designing or my music or my fantasiometry or something—*anything*.'

'Your friends will remember you.'

'Ah, my friends!' He gave a brief smile which it was impossible to interpret: did it dismiss them, as of really no account, or did it acquiesce in the view that, in the end, one's friends were all that mattered? 'Yes, I suppose you will all remember me. But I should have liked something more permanent—I'm afraid that is vain of me, isn't it?'

When we knew that he was dying in a matter of a few hours, Götz refused ever to leave his bedside. Theo would feel for his hand, and sometimes murmur his name, 'Götz' emerging as a curious swallowed croak at the back of the old man's throat. Sometimes Theo would struggle to say something more, but was unable to do so, until, a short time before he passed into unconsciousness, he rallied himself enough to get out: 'Götz . . . this girl . . . don't . . . don't . . . be . . . miserable . . . about her . . . Not . . . worth . . . it . . . George . . . the . . . pastry-cook . . .'

They were the last words he spoke.

I HAVE just been staying with Götz and Kiki in the flat which the Americans have put at their disposal while the excavations are completed and the museum is built. Götz only disposed of the site on the condition that he should be made curator in perpetuity.

Physically, he has changed little, in spite of his marriage: he still gnaws his fingers, his shirt still tends to hang out behind, and his hair still falls in a tangled, platinum fringe across his wide forehead. Kiki herself is already fattening and coarsening. She has lost that pertness which was once her chief attraction, and now seems to face life with a ruminative somnolence which might seem to justify Cecil in always referring to her as 'the Cow'. There were few of Theo's possessions that she wanted for their home and most of them have now passed into the more appreciative hands of his friends (at the back of my kitchen cupboard in Kensington the phallus rests under an upturned paper bag, and the front door of Cecil's Settignano villa is guarded by a Greek military policeman on whose bare thighs the hairs are like the prickles on a cactus).

Götz himself is, I think, sometimes troubled in his conscience. Last night, after Kiki had gone to bed, we found ourselves talking about Theo, and suddenly he asked me: 'Tell me, Frank, do you think it was very wrong of me to agree to having the house pulled down?'

'If it hadn't been pulled down, this temple of Hera would never have been discovered.'

'But that's not the point,' he said; and I, of course, had known that it was not the point. 'You see, I didn't *know* about the temple, did I? When I agreed, it was in order that Dino's brother could put up a block of flats. . . . And after all,' he added, 'Theo had struggled along all those years on nothing but his pension in order to prevent just that happening.'

'Well, it's turned out all right,' I tried to soothe him.

'But what could I do? I had nothing to offer Kiki, and quite rightly her father wouldn't hear of her marrying me until I was financially secure. . . . And she, of course, couldn't understand why, if I had the house, I wouldn't agree to sell it. . . .' He sighed. 'It was very difficult.'

'A pity that the temple had to be to Hera,' I remarked flippantly. 'Not a goddess with whom Theo would have had much sympathy, I feel.'

Götz shook his head moodily: 'I feel I've done wrong. I ought never to have done it.'

'But think of the discovery! There's been nothing like it in Greece since the time of Schliemann.'

But I had said this only to encourage him, and at heart I knew, as he did, that Theo would never have approved. I was remembering our old friend's contemptuous fury against the American excavations when we had taken Mabel Aaronson on a tour of the Agora: 'Philistines!' he had hissed. 'If you knew what beautiful old houses had covered this whole slope. All pulled down for the sake of a few battered columns and a potsherd or two!'

Was it possible to conceive that he would have considered the destruction of his own house any more justified?

'I'm insisting, of course, that the Museum should be called "The Grecos Museum". He'd like that, wouldn't he?'

'Yes, he'd like to be remembered—he always wanted that.'

There was a sad irony, I thought, in Theo's name being perpetuated in this posthumous fashion, after all his abortive strivings after fame—as a dress designer, as a composer, as the only fantasiometrist in the world—while he still lived.

Suddenly I looked across at Götz, slumped conscience-stricken and moody in the hideous chair opposite me.

'Götz, you are happy?' I asked on an impulse.

'Very, very happy.'

He said the words with an emphasis that left not a vestige of doubt.

'Then that seems to me to be a complete justification. Theo would never want more.'

Götz hesitated, gnawing at a knuckle, until: 'He was fond of me, I think—don't you?' he at last got out, slowly and tentatively.

'Yes, he was fond of you.'

That it should be necessary for him to seek this confirmation seemed to me the saddest irony of all.

Also in Gay Modern Classics:

Francis King
A DOMESTIC ANIMAL
UK £3.50/US $6.50
(hardback UK £7.95/US $15.00)

James Purdy
EUSTACE CHISHOLM
AND THE WORKS
UK £3.50/US $6.50
(hardback UK £7.95/US $15.00)

James Purdy
NARROW ROOMS
UK £3.95/US $7.50
(hardback UK £9.95/US $18.95)

André Gide
CORYDON
UK £3.95
(hardback UK £9.95)

John Lehmann
IN THE PURELY
PAGAN SENSE
UK £3.95/US $7.50
(hardback UK £9.95/US $18.95)

T. C. Worsley
FELLOW TRAVELLERS
UK £3.95/US $7.50
(hardback UK £9.95/US $18.50)

Edward Carpenter
TOWARDS
DEMOCRACY
UK £5.95/US $10.95
(hardback UK £17.50/US $32.50)

Edward Carpenter
SELECTED WRITINGS
VOL. 1: SEX
UK £5.95/US $10.95
(hardback UK £17.50/US $32.50)

Our full catalogue is available on request from
GMP Publishers Ltd, P O Box 247, London N15 6RW.
In North America please order from Alyson Publications Inc.,
40 Plympton St, Boston, MA 02118.